One Bad Break

Barry Minnett Jr.

Dedication

I wrote this book for my four boys: Barry Minnett III, Jaylen Barry Minnett, Carter J. Minnett, and Jedidiah B. Minnett.

However, I would like to dedicate this book to my parents, Barry Minnett and Doris Jean "Jeanie" Minnett.

Acknowledgment

First of all, I would like to thank my wife for being so understanding and putting up with me for over twenty-five years now.

I would also like to thank each one of my kids. They may not know it, but they motivated me to finish this book and to be a better man.

I would like to thank my sister, who always has my back and encourages everything I do.

About the Author

I didn't set out to become a writer, but I've always been committed to making a difference in the lives of young people. This book was born out of that commitment. It's my way of reaching beyond the gym floors and community centers to speak directly to the hearts of young men who might be standing at a crossroads.

Over the years, I've had the privilege of volunteering at my local Boys and Girls Club, running an AAU basketball program, and bringing back the Midnight Basketball League, creating a safe space where young men and women could connect, compete, and grow. Every practice, every late-night game, every conversation has been part of a bigger mission: to guide, mentor, and motivate the next generation.

This book continues that mission. It's filled with hard truths, real stories, and honest advice because I believe every young man deserves the chance to make better choices and build a better future.

Thank you for allowing me to share a piece of that journey with you.

— *Barry Minnett*

Father. Mentor. Community Builder. Author.

Preface

I started writing this book to print five copies at the library. Four for my boys and one for my parents. I procrastinated so long that both of my parents passed before I finished the book. However, with the support of my wife, sister, and children, I was encouraged to finish this book.

Although I wrote this book for my boys, I want this book to help any young man make better decisions.

Table of Contents

Dedication i

Acknowledgment ii

About the Author iii

Preface iv

Chapter 1: Killing It 1

Chapter 2: The Beginning 5

Chapter 3: Learning the Game 14

Chapter 4: Redefining My Game 23

Chapter 5: High School Ball 32

Chapter 6: One Bad Break 57

Chapter 7: Me vs Me 60

Chapter 8: AK 67

Chapter 9: No Change 69

Chapter 10: Time for Change 74

Chapter 11: Two of a Kind 78

Chapter 12: Who Does That? 90

Chapter 13: The Good Life 93

Chapter 14: Slow Down 101

Chapter 15: Real Change 110

Chapter 16: The Comedy Show 116

Chapter 17: Gambling 122

Chapter 18: Ball is Back 125

Chapter 19: Tiny 132

Chapter 20: Joe Jackson 137

Chapter 21. Lessons Beyond the Court 139

Chapter 22. Lost Control 157

Chapter 23. Real Change? 164

Chapter 24. Last Chapter 170

Chapter 1: Killing It

The year was 2000, and I was on top of it. I was killing it. Money? Good. Family? Good. My team? Good. That might come off as cocky, but I was a confident young man trying to get it. Since I was getting it, I decided to get away for a few days to see my homeboy, Marcus, in Chicago.

We went to junior high and high school together. He was originally from Indiana, but after college, he stayed in Chicago, so he knew a little bit about the city.

Now, Chicago was about a three-hour drive, and I gotta add—I got high as hell before getting on the road. Marcus was going to plug me when I got there, and I didn't like to ride like that without potential gain.

Once I touched down, we made a quick stop so I could get right before we headed out to the Sky Box. Now this place had it all. I didn't know whether to call it a strip club or Dave & Buster's. There was so much to play with, you could get lost in the ambiance. You name it, it was there. It was like the O.J. Simpson defense team of fantasies.

Needless to say, it was the best.

I don't want to beat a dead horse, but this place had an all star cast of strippers. All I kept thinking to myself was, *I have to get up here more often.*

One dancer came, then another, and another. Every time I came back from the VIP room, my man Marcus had another one waiting for me. So I'd take her back to the VIP. At one point, he even had two girls waiting. I can't remember if they were kissing or not, but I do know I didn't want it to end.

After rapping with girl after girl—sometimes two at a time—I came back to the table and finished my drink. I was feeling good about my decision to get away for a few days. I mean, the women were friendly, the green was loud, and I still had money that I brought just to blow.

It was getting late, and we decided to hit up another spot before ending the night at Harold's Chicken. After a night of drinking, that Harold's was the perfect nightcap to a perfect night.

Marcus had to work early the next morning, so he was up and out. While he was at work, I needed to find something to get into. So I got myself together, rolled a couple for the road, and headed for downtown. Money had been very good to me lately, so in my mind, I had no limits.

You could find me in stores like Prada and La Perla. The new me went to shop, not just to look. So there was a good chance I picked up a couple of things while I was out.

These moments to myself always had me reflecting on my lifestyle. Although I was a "drug dealer" and probably came off like one, the weed smell I brought around with me didn't bother me at this point. I was very secure in who I was.

While driving around downtown Chicago alone (and smoking), I decided to check in back home to make sure everything was good. Before I could make a call, my man Adam called and told me it had been a great weekend and he had people waiting.

I could hear the excitement in his voice.

He said, "Man, I had plenty before you left, and I sold that—and I could move another five this weekend."

He kept asking, "When are you coming home?"

"I told him I wasn't sure and to give me a few, and I'd call him back. Then, I decided to check with other members of my team—and I got the same results. Everyone was either out or just about to run out.

Some I had fronted. Some had paid cash. But at that moment, I had at least ten thousand worth of weed I had fronted before I left—and some more opportunities with Adam waiting—so I decided to go back home the next morning.

That evening, when Marcus got off work, I explained the situation to him. He told me we needed to hit a spot or two that night.

Of course, I was with it, but honestly, all I could think about was how much money was waiting for me back home.

We went to one more club and had a beer, and then I told him I was ready to go. I knew I had a long drive ahead, and I wanted to be halfway rested before hitting the road in the morning.

Usually, I would get high as hell before getting on the road instead of carrying weed with me. That's what I did on the way up there—and it worked out fine.

But against my better judgment, I decided to roll something for the road.

It's funny what happens when you aren't focused.

I was blinded by the money and the potential gain at home. Not only did I smoke that blunt on the way back, but I didn't even think to get something to kill the weed smell. All I could think about was how fast I could get back to the money.

I had a decent amount of gas, and my phone wouldn't stop ringing, so I was now doing 85 in a 55. I'd worked this highway many times and really knew better than to be speeding.

I was on the lookout—but it was too late now.

In the rearview, I saw the flashing lights.

Everything changed in that moment—instantly. I felt my chest tighten, my stomach twist. There's a difference between doing dirt and getting caught in the middle of it. That difference was now closing in behind me, red and blue.

But I'm getting ahead of myself.

Let me take you back to the beginning.

Chapter 2: The Beginning

I was born and raised in Terre Haute, Indiana, by my mom, Millie Rose Mitchell, and my dad, Bernie Madden. My mother was from Terre Haute, Indiana, and my father was born in Louisville, Kentucky. They were married in 1975 and remain together to this day.

Shanon is my older sister, and she lost her twin, Dania, when they were only three months old. Heart issues. As I got older, I truly believed Dania was watching over me when I got myself into some situations.

My parents did everything they could to provide my sister and me with a good life. My father was a mailman for over twenty-five years. My mother worked as a teacher's assistant, and she also did some factory work. We weren't rich (far from it), probably not even middle class. We struggled like everyone else, but my parents would work overtime to keep food on the table, nice clothes on our backs, give us video game systems, and other things kids would want. We were raised with good values and morals. We were good kids.

We did most of our activities as a family. My sister and I didn't spend the night at our friends' houses. In fact, the only place we were allowed to stay was with family. I would spend the night with some of my cousins, but for the most part, I was at home with my family.

When my mother was young, my grandfather would tell her she had a bed when she would ask to spend the night with a friend. My mom would say the same thing to us.

We were sheltered as kids. We weren't allowed to watch certain things on television, and we had to turn our heads when the "bad" parts came on. Some kids in the neighborhood would walk a few blocks to a corner store at nine or ten years old, and we weren't able to go until we got older.

As I look back on my childhood, I'm glad I was sheltered as a child and young man. If I had more freedom, I probably would have done a lot more—and gotten myself in trouble—if I had the opportunities some of my friends had.

At a young age, Pops and I would always watch basketball games on the weekend. We would watch some during the week, but Mom had us in bed by like eight, so not too many late games for me. Bird, Magic, Jordan, and, of course, Dr J—we loved to watch the greats. But who didn't?

People would come through to enjoy the games at our spot, and I got to kick it with the grown men. I always thought it was funny when they would say a "bad word" because of a play and then apologize to me. I enjoyed getting the high-five because of a big play our team just made. It was like I was one of the guys.

Even though it was cool when we had company, I learned more when it was just me and Pops. He would teach me the ins and outs of the game. He also knew he had my full attention (well, as much as I could give him at such a young age). I like to think of it as mental reps. We all know how important reps are in whatever we do. Pops was feeding me those at a young age, and I didn't know it—but he did.

He knew I would have a higher basketball IQ than the average kid my age. I would go on to use those teaching tools myself when I became a father. And as I grew older, so did the appreciation.

My father, being from Louisville, gave me mental reps every time the Cardinals played on television. Ever since I can remember, I have wanted to be a Cardinal. I wanted to wear the red, white, and black! I wanted to play for Denny Crum.

Of course, I wanted to be a Cardinal to make Pops proud of me. When he was there, I would do my best. I would try even harder than if he wasn't there.

See, I idolize my father—and I am an extension of him. So if he liked Louisville, then I loved Louisville.

Watching the games was cool and all, but as soon as I could throw a ball to the rim, my dad had me at the park shooting hoops together. Pops would shoot with me, and all I could think was, *I want to shoot like him!*

After school, I would have to do what little homework I had and wait for Pops to get there so we could go to the park. It was like time was standing still. Pops didn't get off until four-thirty or five o'clock. So while I was watching cartoons (and probably arguing with my older sister about nothing), I couldn't stop looking at the clock, wondering when my dad would walk through the door.

Mom knew when he would be coming, so as the time got closer, she would sit on the porch and let us play out front. I had my ball, dribbling up and down the block when I saw my Pops pull up. I would run toward him, give him a big hug, and ask if we could go shoot. He would smile and tell me we could in a few minutes.

I didn't know why he would need a few minutes before taking me to the park. However, I am a working, married man with kids now, so I know exactly why he had to take a few minutes when he got off work. But without fail, he would come out a few minutes later, ask if I was ready, and off we went.

I fell in love with the game of basketball. Pops and I were putting in some time at the park almost every day. But that still wasn't enough.

I gave up the cartoons (for the most part) and started playing outside while waiting for Pops to get off work. I would shoot the ball into the steps leading up to our house. If the ball came right back, it was a made basket. If it was raining outside, I would shoot on the porch. And if the weather was too bad outside, I would be in the basement putting in work!

I worked up a sweat playing by myself. Counting down from five as I (Dr J) took Magic, Bird, Barkley, or any of the greats to the basket—or hit the game-winner over one of them.

When that guy named Michael Jordan came into the league, I was him. In my mind, anyway.

I would still be playing against the greats, but now I was Mike! When I would return upstairs, my mom would ask me if the game was over and if I won. I would smile at her and say yes. Then I had to explain how I won with the last-second shot. She would congratulate me with a big smile.

From that moment on, I had my biggest fan.

Anyone who knows my mother knows she will kill over her babies.

I can recall one late fall afternoon—my mom and I were headed west on Walnut Street when a truck struck her side of the car. If she asked me once, she asked me one hundred times if I was okay. And I was. I felt fine. Plus, I had a basketball game later that evening, and I wanted to play.

The police were called. They made a report, and we were on our way. My mother went to the hospital, where they put a neck brace on her. I wasn't sure if my mother would make the game or not.

After the hospital, we went home for about thirty minutes before it was time to leave for the game. To my surprise, my mother was up and ready to go. You could tell she was in some pain, but it didn't stop her from going.

That game was something else. Anyone who knows me and how I played knows I shot my share of shots on the court. Sometimes other parents would have something to say about it.

Well, on this particular night, a lady started in on me during the game. (I have to mention that my father was an assistant coach at this time. So my mom and sister were in the crowd, I was on the court, and my dad was on the bench.)

This lady just kept going on and on about me. Mom had enough. She told the lady that I was her son and she shouldn't talk about me. A shot or two later, that lady couldn't help herself. She went in on me again, and my mom went in on her. They were arguing back and forth.

My coach called a time-out, and my father went over to calm my mother down.

Many people know this story. However, this isn't the only time my mother would fight for me—plus I'm her baby. I'm grown now, and she will still kill for us. Or at least try.

Every time I got in trouble in school, she was there. She always told me if I told her the truth, she would defend me. And she did! My mother is the strongest woman I've ever met.

But back to sports.

My first organized basketball experience came when I was in the second grade at the local YMCA. With the knowledge I'd received from Pops and the practice I put in, I was more advanced than the kids at the Y.

I can still remember dribbling up the court, hearing the pounding of the ball as I made my way up the court. The sun was shining in through the window, leaving a shadow on the court. Some parents were cheering, and others were yelling to pass the ball. But like my favorite player, I thought I should get my share of shots.

It didn't hurt that I was about a head taller than most of the kids I played with. So even when I wasn't shooting, I was rebounding and putting it back in.

The Y had a short season, though. I wanted to play more, Pops wanted me to play more, and against some better competition—so the next year he signed me up to play at the Boys Club.

For Christmas that year, I got my first "real" Nerf basketball goal for my room. I had the little goals you could hang from the door, and everything—the goal was the size of a basketball, and the ball was the size of an apple.

This goal was different. I could actually shoot the ball with two hands. I could dunk without running into the door. This one also had a picture of Dr J and his signature on it.

Whenever I had free time, I was on my goal. Right after school until bath and bed, I was playing basketball.

I loved to dunk. Because I would rather dunk than shoot, Pops took the goal off the stand and nailed it to the corner of the wall. Mom wasn't very happy, but Pops got away with it.

Still catching as many games as possible and playing every day, my love for the game grew more than ever.

When it was time to start the season at the Boys Club, I was ready. Third grade, and still about a head taller than most of the kids my age, I was having success at the Boys Club. I really made a name for myself.

I was still taking my share of shots. Being one of the tallest kids on the court, I could get rebounds and put-backs as well. I also brought the ball up the court, so I would often just take my man to the basket.

I thought I loved basketball before, but now I had taken it to a whole new level.

I dreamed about basketball. Not just playing the game, but everything that came with being a star. I didn't just want to play the game, I wanted to be like the greats. I had dreams of me being interviewed with my gold chains on like Dr J. Wanted to be asked what it was like to make that big shot to win the game. I wanted the fancy cars and the pretty women. I wanted the fame and everything that went with it.

Although I was only in the third grade, I did have a second hobby—and that was the ladies.

We were standing in line one day waiting to go outside, and a friend of mine dared me to grab this young lady's backside. I did it—and she told. I was scared my mother and father were going to kill me, so when they asked, "Bernie, did you touch her backside," I replied that I didn't.

Since I had to lie to my parents, I figured I should stop touching girls at school. Well, at least while I was in elementary school. Junior high and high school were another story.

During recess, though, I would play basketball, which meant trying to recruit some people to play with me. Of course, I asked my "friends" first, but they would rather chase the girls around the playground and "accidentally" touch one of them.

When they rejected my invitation to play ball, they would invite me to chase the girls with them. Once I rejected their invite, they would laugh at the fact I would rather play ball than chase girls.

I would laugh too, and just think how one day I would be in the NBA.

Chapter 3: Learning the Game

Fourth grade was the real turning point of my basketball career. Before fourth grade, you could sign up at the local Boys Club and be placed on a team. However, the fourth grade had a draft, and coaches picked their players.

I was chosen by a coach named Ben. Ben helped me develop my game by letting me be free on the court. He didn't hinder me at all. I could try the things my father was working on with me. I could learn by trial and error instead of worrying about someone yelling at me for shooting the ball too much.

We really didn't have the strongest team, so that could have been why Ben allowed me to do me on the court. For me, this paid off big. My confidence on the court grew and grew. I was starting to think I was unstoppable.

The Boys Club had a rule where one player couldn't score more than twenty points a game, unless you were fouled—then you could shoot the free throws. This didn't help us win games, but we were able to compete with the best teams up there. I was either at twenty or knocking at the door in the third quarter. We didn't win the championship that year, but I definitely made a name for myself.

After the season was over, it was time to put more work in.

One night, I asked if Pops could dunk, and he said yes. And then he did! I didn't know my Pops could get up like that. So I asked to see another—and another.

After about five or so dunks, Pops came down, and I knew something wasn't right. He grabbed his back, and I could see the pain on his face.

He looked at me and said, "We have to go."

Pops wasn't just the strongest person I knew—he was my hero. Seeing him in so much pain really hurt me. I also felt it was my fault since I kept asking him to dunk.

After gathering our things, we headed home, and Pops couldn't even walk straight. He walked bent over all the way home. Mom didn't waste any time helping Pops get into the car so she could take him to the emergency room.

Pops had suffered a slipped disc and had to be off work for six months.

Although Pops was now unable to take me to the park and work out with me, I was in the fifth grade and arguably the best in my age group. If I wasn't, I was one of them. I averaged close to twenty points a game. There were many games where I could only score free throws in the fourth quarter because I had already hit the twenty-point limit.

Ben was my coach again. That year, he asked my dad to help him coach to make sure no one else could draft me.

At the end of the season, an all star team was being put together, and the people selected would compete against other all star teams around the state. After being one of the league's leading scorers for my age group, I thought I had a very good chance of making this team.

During tryouts, I went hard. This was my chance to prove to everyone that I was one of the best. Although I was not really into the running part of practice, I ran my hardest. I went as hard as possible in every drill.

After a couple of days of tryouts, they posted a list—and I was on it!

Practice would be my chance to show the coaches what I could really do. The first couple of days, we just did drills and not much scrimmaging. Pops always told me not to take shortcuts and to work as hard as possible because someone could be watching.

Figuring someone was seeing how hard I was going, I thought they would give me the chance to start—or at least be the sixth man.

However, toward the end of the week, we were learning plays and scrimmaging against each other. I didn't know how this coach was doing things, since I was used to the first five to learn the plays usually being the starters.

I was confused now because I was not in that first five. Pops told me not to worry about starting and to prove myself when I got a chance.

However, that chance never came.

I sat on the bench the whole all star season. I might have gotten in the game with fifty-five seconds left when we were already getting killed.

The disappointment that I wasn't given a chance didn't stop me from wanting to get better and prove myself the next year.

Sixth grade was not much different from fifth grade. I had the same coach, and I was still averaging close to twenty points a game.

At the last game of the season, we were playing a team from Sullivan (a small town just south of us). We were winning the game, so with about one minute left, my coach told me to hold the ball to get fouled or run the clock out. So that's what I was doing.

I was being guarded by the starting point guard for the all star team that we played on the previous year. He was having a tough time staying in front of me because I was putting move after move on him. This dude couldn't guard me, and I was going to let everyone see it! I tried to make him look as bad as possible.

Before the game was over, during my dribbling expedition, the referee called a timeout. This was crazy because if no one needed to tie their shoes, the referees didn't call timeouts.

The referee called a timeout to pull me to the side to tell me NOT to do my all star teammate like that.

I was confused. Why not? I didn't play. I sat on the bench. He started. If he can't hold me, why was he starting? Why wasn't I starting?

Well, I never got an answer to that question, because when the all star season started, I was once again a benchwarmer—still only getting a few seconds every now and then.

I told my Pops I didn't want to play anymore. I just wanted to quit and wait until next year to play for my junior high school team. Pops and Mom wouldn't let me quit. My parents had to pay for us to travel. They were spending money, and they were also upset I wasn't playing. However, they told me if I started something, I was going to finish.

The all star season finally ended. I thought I would never be happy about that, but not getting playing time really bothered me.

I was older now, so I could go to school by myself and just play. My parents would also let me go to another park down the street. I was determined never to sit on the bench again.

As a sixth grader, I didn't have the best grades. I just wanted to play basketball. My parents would say you have to have something to fall back on. *What if basketball didn't work out?*

In my mind, basketball WOULD work out, so I just needed grades good enough to play ball.

Halfway through the year, we got a transfer student, Derrick. While I didn't know why he transferred, I was glad he was there. He was African American like me. I assumed he would be like me.

I couldn't have been more wrong.

Derrick was very mature for his age, although he looked even younger than he really was. He hung out on the streets. He would come to school and tell me about things that were going on in the streets. We would never have a normal sixth-grade conversation.

He knew about things I would overhear my parents talking about. I would question him daily, and he would answer like he was my teacher.

He asked me if I wanted to make some money. I said yes, since he always seemed to have a couple of dollars in his pocket. He told me we could sell our pens, pencils, and anything else that was new or looked new.

Derrick and I were sitting by each other in class at this time, and we were having indoor recess because of the weather. So we just put our desks together and put all our merchandise on top of our desks.

My mom always overdid it with the school supplies, so I had many new things that I wasn't using, and they were all for sale.

Our teacher didn't say anything, but we did get a visit from the principal. He walked in with a smirk on his face as he looked at our setup. He told us he had to see this little shop he had heard about. He also let us know if it got too big, he would have to shut it down.

As smart as Derrick was, he never thought we needed to buy more supplies so we could sell. So once we sold everything, the shop was closed.

School was out for the summer, and next year I'd be in junior high school. There was no reason for me to be nervous like some of the other kids. Shanon was already there, and so were some kids from the Boys Club.

I was more focused on getting to the NBA.

Pops told me this year would be different. He told me this coach wants to win. As long as I work hard, I will get to play—and he assured me it wouldn't be like the all stars.

I still played ball every chance I got over the summer. We would go to the Boys Club and play in the open gym.

One Saturday, the Boys Club was having a slam dunk contest and a three point shootout. This was an opportunity for me to have some fun and also show off a little bit.

Of course, I had to call my biggest fan and tell her I was about to be in a dunk contest and three point shootout. She was there in about five minutes.

Before any game I played, I had to spot my mom and dad. It gave me a sense of comfort on the court. My mom would be at every game and probably the loudest parent in the crowd. My Pops was at every game possible. He worked some Saturdays, so he missed a game or two. He was working this Saturday and was unable to get off, but I spotted my mom before I took my turn in the three point shootout.

Just before I took my first shot, I heard her cheering—but then I zoned out. Knocking down shot after shot, I won the three point shootout.

Now I had to get signed up for the slam dunk contest.

I loved to dunk and never got a chance, so I thought I would just have a little fun with it. Honestly, I can't remember what my first two dunks were. While watching the other competitors from the bleachers, I didn't know what I was going to do for my last dunk. I was still not sure even as my name got called.

As I walked up to get the ball, I happened to look at the judges, and there was an extra chair. The light bulb went off in my head.

I asked if I could use the chair, and one of them asked if I was sure. With a big smile on my face, I shook my head yes. I wanted to put the chair on the free-throw line and really end it with a bang. However, I decided against that, put it in the middle of the lane, and slowly walked back past half-court.

I took off, took a few dribbles as I headed toward the chair. I cleared the chair easy—and the crowd went crazy.

Although I got a good reception on my last dunk, I didn't think I would win the contest. It really didn't matter since I was more concerned with winning the three point shootout.

I found a friend of mine sitting in the bleachers. I made my way up to where he was, shook his hand, and sat down. We began a little small talk, and they began to announce the winner for our age group. They started with the runner-up—and it wasn't me. I figured I wouldn't get it, but I was okay with not winning.

My homey looked at me and said, "You know you won," and at the same time, they announced that I had won the dunk contest.

I stayed after the event. We ran a few games before I went home, but I couldn't wait to get home and tell my Pops that I had won both the three-point shotout and dunk contest.

Since my mom had already left, I knew she would tell him before I got home—but I told him anyway, as if he had no idea.

Pops was good at keeping me focused. Although I had a good day at the Boys Club, I still had to keep putting in work if I was gonna play junior high basketball.

Thinking back, I think I would have made the team anyway. But Pops always told me not to be too confident and to prove myself.

So that's what I did.

I worked hard over the summer and prepared myself for junior high basketball.

The game had always been there. Now, I was just learning how to truly chase it.

Chapter 4: Redefining My Game

Junior high basketball was different from Boys Club basketball. In junior high, it was all about winning the county championship.

Our junior high school had won the county championship the year before, and we had a strong team, so we were expected to win as well.

Jordan Park coached us. He was one of my favorite coaches and by far one of the best. One of the things that I took from him, even when I became a coach myself, was his no-nonsense approach. Coach Park didn't allow us to play around. Things had to be done his way—or you didn't play. But he was a winner!

He won multiple county championships and helped prepare many players for high school basketball. He had the right people shooting the ball, ran the right plays at the right time, and knew how to communicate with his players.

I can remember him not letting us shoot the three-point shots for the first couple of games.

One game, with three or so seconds on the clock while the other team was shooting a free throw, he yelled at me, "Bernie, get over here!" I thought I did something wrong. When I ran over to him, he said, "Stand right here. We're going to get you the ball, and I want you to shoot it."

They missed the free throw, so our big man got the rebound and threw it to me up the court. I shot and hit my first three-pointer—behind the volleyball line—as the buzzer went off.

That was just the beginning of a good seventh-grade year (on the basketball court). My grades were still average. Nothing to brag about, but I was always eligible to play basketball.

I had played with the guys in the grade above me many times, and I could hang with them like I was their age. So that summer, I went to a camp with some guys from Wilson's eighth-grade team. It was a team camp, but we also did individual drills.

It was a week-long camp, and I was homesick the first couple of days. On the third or so night, things got interesting.

I went into my teammates' room, and they were playing cards. They weren't just playing for fun—they were betting money on the game. I really wanted to stay and play, even though I knew we were supposed to be in our own rooms since it was getting close to curfew.

Against my better judgment, I decided to stay and play. I couldn't pass up the chance to win some money. I wasn't doing bad for myself—I had won a few hands and made some money.

We were all having a good time when we heard someone knock on the door. It was an older man (the RA). He was supposed to make sure we were all in our rooms by a certain time.

When we heard the knock, everyone started to shove their money into the desk drawers. There was no way I was putting my money in there. Although we were in my teammates' room, I didn't feel like I would get my money back if it came down to it.

I decided to put my dollars in my sock while dropping the change into my shoe instead.

There were only three players from my team in the room. The other two stayed there besides me. So one of the players jumped into the bed and pretended to sleep, and the other opened the door.

The RA walked in and asked what was going on. My teammate, who opened the door, started telling him we were just talking basketball.

It didn't matter. Since we weren't in our rooms, we were told to go with him.

I had no idea where we were going, and I was worried about my coach finding out. Worse, I knew he would tell my parents, and I would be in deep trouble.

They walked us to the track to run laps because we were not where we were supposed to be. When we got there, it was sprinkling. We ran a lap, and the rain started to come down—not really hard, but enough to make it miserable.

To make it worse, I was running with change in my shoe, stabbing my foot with every step.

We ran a mile and were sent back to our rooms afterward. Although I didn't enjoy running with change digging into my foot I was glad my coach never found out—and I kept my money.

Later, I found out that the other guys took the money from players on other teams who had hidden their cash in the drawers.

After camp that summer, I played some at the parks and at the open gym at the high school I would eventually attend.

During the last month of the summer, my parents thought it would be good for my sister and me to detassel corn, so they signed us up. I didn't mind because I wanted to make some money. We had to be up at about 3:30 a.m. to fix lunch and make it to the bus pickup at 5 a.m.

We got paid for the ride to the cornfields but not the ride home. It would take an hour or so to get there. The corn was wet in the morning, so we wore long-sleeve shirts. By the time lunch came, it was very hot. It was not a dream job by any means. However, I was going to be able to buy myself some Jordan gear I had spotted in a local shoe store.

We made probably four or five hundred dollars that summer, and I bought myself a Jordan sweatsuit and a pair of Jordan shoes. I saved the rest of the money.

I started school that year with a little bit of cash in my pocket.

Eighth grade wasn't the same as seventh. Coach Park wasn't coaching us. Even though our new coach was good, I wanted Coach Park back. We had a good player-coach relationship.

Our team was still the strongest in the county, but early in the season, we lost to a rival school. That game was crazy! It was standing room only, and the crowd was going wild. We were on the road, and it was a close game until the end. We even went into overtime.

I fouled out in the fourth quarter, so I didn't get to play in overtime.

That was the only loss we suffered in the two years I played at Wilson. I was among the top three scorers in a season for both seventh and eighth grade.

I can only remember one other game that year. After a win (I can't remember who we played), we went to our locker room, which was actually the weight room, and all my clothes were gone.

I just happened to wear the sweatsuit that I bought with my own money. Not only was my sweatsuit gone, but my Jordans were gone too. I wore my father's Bulls jacket that day—and it was gone as well.

The door had been left unlocked, and some kids came in and stole things.

The school kept the uniforms, so after the game, I had to wait for my parents to go home and get me some clothes so I could leave. The stolen items were never returned to me, but my parents did replace them.

Before AAU basketball started, I played in a summer league at North High School. I played well, and my game was really coming around.

I remember staying after one practice to shoot while waiting for my parents. The coach pulled out a device that measured your vertical jump. You put a ball on top, and you try to knock it loose.

After I finished, he moved it up to the rim, right at the top of the square on the backboard.

He told me I was a good ballplayer and encouraged me to keep working.

When my parents arrived, he asked to speak to them briefly, however it took an hour, trying to get them to send me to North instead of South. He told them how well I played and said he thought I could probably play some varsity as a freshman.

But I didn't play there. I was in the South district— so South it was.

The summer after eighth grade was the first time I was introduced to AAU basketball. My coach from the Boys Club, Ben, told my parents and me about it, and I played my first summer of AAU basketball.

There wasn't a twenty-point rule like at the Boys Club. I could score as much as possible, and I did.

I had numerous twenty-plus games that summer. I was on a team Ben put together. It wasn't the strongest, but I was able to show my abilities.

I always had somewhat of an attitude, but as I got older, it got worse. I myself started to notice it during this AAU season.

I can remember being at a tournament and Ben telling me, "No one can stop you but you." He went on to say no one on the court could guard me. But if I had an attitude, I was stopping myself from being the best player I could be.

(This was something my parents would continue to remind me throughout my career.)

We played a few tournaments that summer, including the state tournament. The scores were recorded in the local newspaper. My best tournament came in May of 1990. The paper read:

The Terre Haute boys 14-and-under AAU basketball team was 1-2 at the Anderson Shootout in Anderson on Saturday. Wabash AAU defeated Terre Haute AAU 77-71 in the first game, with Bernie Madden scoring 28 points. In the second game, Terre Haute defeated Decatur 82-76, behind Madden's 28 points. Terre Haute was eliminated from the tournament by Witko 81-76 despite 43 points from Madden.

We finished in the top eight that year. I scored twenty-six points in the opening round of the state tournament, which we won 63-58. In the second round, I scored thirty-six points in a 75-50 win. In the next game, I scored twenty-six points in a 75-63 win. We lost the following game 86-51, but I still managed twenty-two points.

I changed my hustle once again in eighth grade. I knew a couple of kids who were stealing cassette tapes and CDs from K-Mart. They were selling to everyone.

At first, I thought I would purchase some and resell them myself, but then an idea popped into my head.

I told them I would buy all their tapes for a lower price and be the only one they had to sell to.

That worked until they were no longer able to get the tapes and CDs.

For some reason, I felt like I could sell anything. Anything I could get at a discount, I would get and flip. We weren't poor, so I didn't need to do this. My parents gave me lunch money and also a few dollars to get something to eat before the games. But I was always looking for ways to have a little more in my pocket.

One day (during basketball season), I was sitting in the class I had right before lunch and struck up a conversation with a quiet kid who sat across from me. Gabe.

During that conversation, I asked if his dad owned the business that shared his last name, and he said yes. If I'm not mistaken, he said his grandfather owned it and passed it down.

Gabe began opening up more and asking his own questions. He knew I was on the team, and when he asked what I thought would happen that night, I confidently said, "We'll win, and I'll score twenty."

I also learned how to "borrow" money.

I would tell Gabe I didn't have lunch money. I would explain that I had practice or a game that night without anything to eat. Feeling bad for me, he would loan me a dollar or two almost every day.

His father owned a business, so he always had between five and ten dollars on him.

This was my way of eating lunch—and keeping my lunch money.

I even turned a couple of my friends onto the idea, and we took it to the extreme.

One night at the school "fun club" (a dance we had about four or five times a year), we asked everyone to borrow money. Some kids said they didn't have a dollar, so we would take whatever they were willing to give us.

That night, I ended up with about fourty dollars.

Some of the guys on the team saw what we were doing and started to do it too.

Things went bad after that.

Someone told on me. One of the teachers pulled me aside and asked what I was doing. He said I had to return all the money or he would tell my parents.

This was my first time getting caught, and I knew my parents would kill me if they found out. Although the thought of getting in trouble bothered me, I knew I was beyond the "butt whooping" stage.

I decided to keep the money and hope he didn't tell.

Luckily, he didn't.

This teacher was cool. He never told my parents— and he never held it against me.

Soon, the season was over.

And it was time to start focusing on the next goal:

High school basketball.

Chapter 5: High School Ball

Freshman year was the most exciting time in my basketball career. This was the first year in Terre Haute that freshmen could play at the high school.

In 1993, the freshmen were moved into the high schools. However, in 1992—the year I was a freshman—the players who were able to play varsity or junior varsity could go to school at their junior high and play sports at the high school.

That summer, I worked on my game even more and prepared for my chance to be one of the first freshmen to play at Terre Haute South. I was dunking now—just a regular one-handed dunk. Not many of the upperclassmen could even do that.

Tryouts came, and I was as ready as I'd ever been. Running sprints, I was in the top three. Drills were no different—top three. But scrimmaging was where I did best. I could score and rebound at this level. To be honest, offensively, I was better than most on that junior varsity team.

Since I played well on the last day of tryouts, the head coach called me over to talk to me. He told me he loved the way I was playing, that I would have to keep working hard, but that they were going to keep me.

If the high school kept you, they had to play you at least two quarters. This made my confidence grow even more. I didn't worry about making mistakes. I played freely.

I would attend my junior high, but then go to practice at the high school. The opportunity humbled me, but things were changing.

There was only one other freshman who played JV—the same guy I had dribbled circles around at the Boys Club when the ref called a time-out.

I started junior varsity and led the team in scoring. I was playing well and thought that I might even get a chance to dress varsity before the season was over.

During practice, we would scrimmage against the varsity team. We had a strong varsity team. There was a guy named Matthew Walls. He was the best player I ever played against—hands down. He could do any dunk you wanted and was just a phenomenal athlete.

I remember being in an open gym the summer before and watching him dunk with a foot inside the free-throw line. He would get a stack of letters from all the big-name schools almost every day. He signed with Indiana before his senior year.

He dunked on me a couple of times when we scrimmaged against the varsity team. I also blocked his shot a few times. I blocked a lot of the upperclassmen's shots, though.

Once, when we were scrimmaging, Matt tried to dunk on me from the box at the bottom of the foul line. I just stood there, not thinking he was actually going to try to dunk from there.

He went up—and we both went down.

He thought I tried to undercut him, so he was very upset. The coaches pulled me out and left him in. I was on the side talking to another player from the junior varsity, laughing and having a good time.

When Matt looked over and saw us laughing, he snapped.

"What are you laughing at? You think it's funny?"

We were on opposite sides of the court. My friend (no longer with us) told me not to worry and said he had my back. I was planning on kicking this dude and running out the door if I had to.

The coaches grabbed him and told me to come down to that end of the court. We talked with the coaches, and the issue was squashed.

I'm not sure if this was the reason I didn't get to dress varsity, but I'm sure having one of the best players on the team want to fight you doesn't help.

Although I didn't get to dress varsity, I started every JV game and led the team in scoring that year.

It was a pretty successful season.

After home games, they would have a dance or party in the cafeteria. Usually, after the games, I would find my parents waiting for me—my mom to tell me how well I played, and my dad to tell me what I did wrong.

Listening to them, I would exit the gym while shaking hands with my teammates as they walked toward the cafeteria.

In one of the last games of the season, I got my first in-game dunk. Of course, I was excited and couldn't wait to talk about it with my father. However, as I was leaving, instead of high fives and handshakes, a couple of the players asked me if I was staying for the dance.

I looked at my parents and asked if I could stay. They both agreed, and my father reached into his pocket to give me some money.

I wasn't much of a dancer, and I didn't know many people there besides the basketball players. I really wasn't having too much fun.

I sat for about an hour, moving from one corner of the room to another. Some of the guys would approach me and joke around for a minute before disappearing.

With about half an hour left, a young lady and her friend approached me. They asked if I was the guy who had just dunked in the JV game. She told me how impressed they both were with my play.

One was more talkative than the other, so after a little more small talk, I asked for her number. She smiled and said she would be right back. She returned with the corner of a piece of paper with her name and number on it.

I reached for the paper with a smile and told her I would call.

We became friends after that, and since she had a car, sometimes I would call and get a ride from her.

Since I was on the high school team, I didn't get many chances to watch my friends play. Although I was on JV and had some success, I missed my friends—the guys I had a chance to play with for the last two years.

Our school made it to the county championship that year, without me. This was the only game I was able to attend.

When I got there, things felt different. I paid to get into the game, which in itself was weird—paying for a game I should have been playing in.

The person at the table asked how it was going at South. I said, 'Good,' and they told me they were happy for me. I smiled and thanked them as they motioned for me to come in.

The game was already underway when I got there—first quarter, and we were winning.

It was still weird being there. As I walked in, I remembered playing in this gym.

And although I missed playing junior high basketball, I wouldn't trade my freshman year for anything.

As I made my way to an open spot in the bleachers, I shook hands with the parents of the guys on my old team, spoke to a few classmates, and then sat to take it all in.

As I watched the game, it seemed different. Slower. I thought I could go out there and score fifty that night.

But I was excited to watch my friends win the county championship.

Even though I was somewhat disappointed that I couldn't help them win or play with them, I was happy with my situation.

The summer before sophomore year was serious for me.

I woke up at 6 a.m. to go to the park and do shooting and ball-handling drills.

I had a good friend who would meet me at the park and work out with me. I really don't know what motivated my friend because he wasn't a ball player.

But he didn't miss a session.

He was there every morning with me, rebounding and actually doing the same drills I was doing.

After about a month of morning workouts, I started jumping "boxes" with another good friend of mine. My friend Marcus played tennis, and his father had him jumping boxes and doing some other drills to make him quicker.

Marcus invited me to their workout, which was also at 6 a.m.

It was difficult. His dad pushed us hard, and after two or three weeks, I was ready to see what it did for me.

Marcus and his father came to watch me play in an AAU game at the Boys Club. I was jumping out of the gym. I got maybe four or five dunks that game. I was now doing whatever dunk I wanted. I was up so high that I would dunk hard and swing on the rim like a monkey.

One of the refs for that game worked with my father at the post office. He told me he loved to watch me dunk but would give me a tech if I kept swinging on the rim.

I was excited to start my sophomore season.

During tryouts, we played three-on-three. Our biggest guy was 6'6" and he was the starting center. He stood in front of the basket, and when the ball came off the rim, I caught it and dunked on him.

Things went well, and I ended up starting in the first game.

I can still remember that game. We played White River Valley on the road. We were down the whole game, and then we came back from sixteen points down, forced overtime, and even got the win.

The newspaper said, "Heroes for South were many, the final one being Sophomore Bernie Madden and his two free throws with five seconds left."

This was my first varsity game, and I was very nervous to shoot those free throws. The tension was clear when I stepped to the line. I shot both of them with all arms—they probably hit every part of the rim before falling in.

After the game, my coach told me I wasn't a sophomore anymore after hitting clutch free throws like that.

Around this time, I also received my first letter—from James Madison University, a D1 school! The letter stated they couldn't send me any information until my junior year because of ISHAA rules. Still, they wanted me to fill out a questionnaire so they could have my information on file and contact me when they could.

I also received a letter from Butler University that year. They said the same thing.

A couple of weeks later, I was playing basketball at school when my parents came to pick me up. They told me we had to go to the newspaper because they wanted to interview me before the rival North-South game.

This was the first time the newspaper interviewed me, but it wouldn't be the last.

I ended that game with eleven points. Our leading scorer had sixteen in a 53-51 loss.

After a couple of bad games, the coach decided to bring me in off the bench.

In the first game off the bench, I had fourteen points, nine rebounds, and three blocked shots.

I can remember scoring ten points in the first quarter against Ben Davis. I figured I'd score forty against one of the best teams in the state, but I was pulled in and out for the rest of the game.

I started getting an attitude.

I was playing well, but my coach refused to keep me on the court. We lost, and I didn't score anymore for the rest of the game. I let my attitude dictate my game.

My parents would remind me of what my first AAU coach, Ben, told me: "No one can stop you but you."

It didn't change my attitude much, though. Plus, I didn't feel like my coach treated me fairly.

A week later, I would lead the team to a 68–63 win with twenty-one points, shooting 4/5 from the three-point line.

The opposing team's coach would say to the newspaper, "Madden kind of surprised us a little bit."

The local newspaper did an article once a week on who they thought was Athlete of the Week. I got the Athlete of the Week following that game. In the article, they said:

"He's been doing it all season, but he really came to the limelight for the first time big time Friday night. Bernie Madden scored a career-high 21 points as Terre Haute South knocked off perennial power Vincennes 68–65 in Braves' homecoming."

I followed with another good game. I scored twenty that game, again going 4/5 from the three-point line.

One of my best games of the season would come a few games later. I led the team with eighteen points, eleven rebounds, five steals, four assists, and a blocked shot.

I also took driver's education at school that year. I actually got a good grade in that class because I really wanted to drive.

I got my license that year and wanted my own car.

After the season, I got a job at Wendy's, where I worked for about six months. My parents had a 1979

Monte Carlo that they gave me; however, it didn't run, and I would have to get it fixed.

It needed some engine work, so I worked overtime at Wendy's. My uncle did the engine work for me, so all I had to do was pay for the parts.

Once I got my car fixed, I was able to drive to and from school. Even better, I was able to hang out with friends more and find different places to play ball.

I had played well my sophomore year and had a couple of different teams I could have played for this AAU season, including a team out of Bloomington, IN.

At six feet tall, I would be the second shortest player on this team. The other players came from different parts of Indiana.

The coach called and told me that with me on the team, he thought we would win the state tournament.

I also had the option to play with a team of local players from around the Terre Haute area. This team was a year older, so I would be playing in a higher grade.

After talking to both coaches, I went with the Bloomington team. Everything sounded real good.

We were getting uniforms like Michigan. We were supposed to have some of the best players in the state, so I thought we would win State.

We would practice once or twice a week in Bloomington.

I would carpool with a guy from West Terre Haute who also played on this team.

I can remember one practice real well.

We started off doing a lay-up line. Since we only had two guys six feet or shorter, it turned into a dunk line.

We had a 6'6" player named Dwayne. He could shoot and jump out of the gym and would later play at Wisconsin University.

He was the team's go-to guy and the reason the team was put together.

Dwayne started the dunk line with basic dunks—one hand, then two hands. Then he got more advanced with the dunks.

I followed him, and whatever he did, I did.

We did 360s, backwards dunks, off the backboard, etc. The coaches were impressed that I could do what he could do since I was only six feet tall.

Once we started to scrimmage, I was on the opposite team from Dwayne. We went at it, and I got the best of him that day.

After that practice, I didn't get the playing time I thought I should have gotten.

We played in the state tournament and placed fourth or fifth, I think. We should have done better, but I thought the coach made too many substitutions. He wanted to save our legs, but we still lost.

A month or two later, I received a call from Nick Hughes.

He asked if we were still playing and, if not, if I would like to play in a tournament in Louisville.

Of course, I still wanted to play, and most of the guys would be seniors, so I figured it would be a great opportunity.

Scouts or colleges didn't matter; I just needed to keep playing.

In the first game we played, I played average. I couldn't tell you how many points I had or any stats from that game.

However, the second game was probably the best game I've played in my life!

My career high was forty-six points. In this game, I only scored twenty-nine, but that's not why it was the best.

I only had one point in the entire first half. The second half was different.

I can still recall being on the court and seeing all the scouts surrounding it. I looked around as if it were in slow motion, reading the scouts' shirts. It seemed like every school in the country was there.

We were playing a team from Virginia, and as I was looking at all the scouts, my man was bringing the ball up the court.

I was waiting on him at half court, standing straight up and down. I was already upset by only having one point. But something told me to play my game.

I smacked the ground, dropped down in my defensive stance, and started playing good defense.

I got a steal and dunked it in.

I was ready.

We were losing at the half, but we were coming back.

We were a team put together just so we could play. We didn't have the expensive uniforms and matching shoes like the team we were playing. We were definitely the underdogs—and we were right there.

There were maybe fifteen seconds left on the clock. Down by two, Nick called a timeout.

He set up a play for me to get the ball.

I got it on the wing with maybe five seconds left. I just pulled up deep for three—and it was over.

I hit the game-winner, but I also had three or four dunks.

I ended the game with twenty-nine points, and twenty-eight of them came in the second half.

We celebrated right after the game, and I remember Nick talking to scouts at the same time.

When we got back to the room, my teammates were having a good time celebrating, but I wanted to talk basketball. So I went and spoke to Nick.

He told me that there were some schools interested in me.

North Carolina, Louisville, and Kansas all liked the way I played.

Nick said Kansas told him they would sign me right now. The scout said I was a guard that could do it all—and that's what they were looking for.

They knew I wasn't going to be a senior like everyone else, though, and said they would contact me.

I never received a letter from any of the big-name schools except for Louisville.

My coach knew I went to Louisville, but he thought it was for a camp.

I recall seeing him in the hallway—there was no one else in the hall, just him and me. He gave me the letter and said that he knew I went to the camp, and they probably wanted me to come back.

I always wondered where he was going and why he had my letter with him.

I had heard from many players who had played at both high schools that the coaches would throw their letters in the trash.

However, when I read the letter from Louisville, it was a letter and a questionnaire for recruits.

Not long after receiving the Louisville letter, I started getting other letters, mainly from D2 and D3 schools.

However, James Madison was showing me a lot of attention.

They were calling me and sending me not only letters, but basketball yearbooks.

I was excited by the recruitment process, but I had made my mind up early that if Louisville would take me, that's where I was going!

I didn't build off my sophomore year like I should have. I played okay, but nowhere near how I should have. I could still dunk, but not like my sophomore year. I could still do the regular dunks—one or two hands, though.

I didn't work out like I should have either. I can recall asking someone to open the gym for us in the morning, and an assistant junior varsity coach did for a couple of days—and that was it. He told us he couldn't come that early anymore.

I did have some good games. I was also the team's leading scorer and rebounder that year.

I was the first to leave the game in almost every game in the first quarter. I couldn't figure out why I was always substituted so early in the game, and it really bothered me.

In one of our first games of the season, I scored eighteen points and grabbed seven rebounds to lead our team to the win.

However, I did do other things to get us that 55–52 win. The newspaper said:

"Madden could have made a game-clinching play when he blocked a potential game-tying three pointer. Then retrieved the ball, drove to the other end, and was fouled. Madden's two free throws gave South a lead."

They did later tie the game at 52–52 with six seconds left when our coach called a timeout. We needed to figure out how to get the ball to our point guard.

So the ball was given to me, and I brought it up and found the point guard, and he hit the game-winning three pointer.

Three days later, we played our rival, Terre Haute North.

I was excited to play this game, which is always played in the Hulman Center, where Indiana State plays.

This was, in my opinion, the best high school game I had played to date. I finished the game with twenty-eight points, shooting 4/6 from the three-point line, and nine rebounds.

I scored the first two baskets and a free throw for my team. Later, I would help break the game open with back-to-back three-pointers.

I would once again get the Player of the Week honors after the North–South rivalry game.

The newspaper article said:

"The Terre Haute South Braves are rising to great heights in the early going of this high school basketball season, in part due to the fine play of Bernie Madden! The 6' junior forward would lead all scorers and rebounders in South's 75–49 demolishing of North last Friday night at the Hulman Center. The returning letterman fired in 28 points and pulled down 9 rebounds as he shot a sizzling 67 percent from the floor. Three nights earlier at Sullivan, Madden scored 18 points and rebounded seven shots, made five steals, and blocked a shot as the Braves nipped the Golden Arrows 55–52. Madden was the man who found Anthony Free and dished to him for the game-winning throw at the buzzer."

My next big game came against an Evansville team a couple of weeks later.

The newspaper said:

"Bernie Madden led all scorers with 24 points and also went to work on the backboards to erase Central's early dominance in that category... South led 41–27 at halftime, then removed all doubts about the outcome by scoring 10 straight points midway through the third quarter for a 58–36 lead. Madden had six of those 10 points, including a rebound basket and a dunk."

My coach would say to the paper:

"Bernie really got us going tonight. He got a lot of rebounds, and because of that, we were able to get some fast breaks."

I finished the game with twenty-four points, eleven rebounds, three assists, and two steals.

I was interviewed by the newspaper the following week because of my play that night.

The title of the article was, *"When Madden keeps his head up, the Braves motor."*

The article opened with:

"There have been times this season when Bernie Madden has been the best high school basketball player in town, equally capable of drilling a series of three-point shots or driving to the basket and dunking. There have also been times when his Terre Haute South team has been the best. Often, those two events happen on the same night, which may not be a coincidence."

In the interview, I said that I had to keep my head up. It didn't matter if I was playing well or not.

I was having issues with my attitude, and some of it was because my game wasn't consistent.

It didn't help that I felt like my coach was pulling me in and out of the game.

In the next game, we won 53-48, and I led the team with twelve points. The newspaper would say, "While Madden was the only South player in double figures with 12 points, one-third of those on a four-point play with 3:40 left in regulation time to cut the lead to 44-43."

We would lose the game 53-48.

The following night, we played the best team in the state at the time. It was a close game until the fourth quarter. The newspaper would say, "After falling behind by seven points early in the second quarter, South put together a 12-2 run sparked by seven points and an assist by Bernie Madden to take a 27-24 lead... If anyone left Saturday's game after three quarters, they'd wonder about the final score themselves. However, it's doubtful anyone who watched the third quarter—with its three lead changes in the first 20 seconds, six in the first two minutes, and 10 in the period—would be surprised."

I led the team in scoring with seventeen that game.

My career high would come later in the year. It was a double-overtime win against an Evansville team.

The newspaper wrote, "Bernie Madden racked up big numbers: 29 points, seven 3-pointers, eight rebounds, and three steals." It continued, "Madden provided his share of heroics too, swishing an off-balance 3-pointer with 22 seconds left in regulation play to tie the score at 59-59."

This game was big to me in more than one way. I was happy to have my career high; however, I knew that the 7 three pointers were a record for a single game.

The games' programs had all of the records in them, and a teacher told me that he would get me the first copy of the new program—the one that would have my record in it. When I was younger and went to South games, I told myself I would make the program one day. The three-point record was the only one broken that year.

Unfortunately, that was also the last year they printed the records in the program.

That year , there was a dunk contest and a three point shootout for high school players. I wanted to enter the three point contest; however, I entered the dunk contest for my team. Since I couldn't palm the ball very well, I had one of our assistant coaches spray something on my hands that was usually used on shoes to help keep from sliding.

Before the contest started, I ran into some guys I played with, and they went to shake my hand. I had to give them a fist bump because I didn't want my hand to stick to theirs. One problem—my fingers were stuck together now.

Luckily, I got them unstuck, and my first two dunks put me in the lead. All I had to do was make my last dunk. I didn't want to advance if I couldn't do something good in the regionals, so I attempted a 360 and missed. Actually, I got hung—so I didn't advance.

Even though I didn't want to advance because I wasn't jumping as high as I was the year before, I was embarrassed.

Every year, the newspaper came up with the All-County team. This year, I was on the second team for the second year in a row. The paper stated, "A second straight award for this 6'1" junior, at times the county's most explosive offensive player and improved rebounder and defender."

I thought I would be on the first team after that year. However, I had an up-and-down year, and my team didn't make it out of the sectionals.

This year (and the only year I can remember), we had female managers. They were really into basketball, but I guess they weren't good enough to play, or they didn't want to.

Anyway, we enjoyed having them around. Well, I won't speak for everyone else. I enjoyed having them around.

I remember being in practice, shooting before practice actually began, with my friend Mark. Mark saw me looking in that direction and asked me which one I wanted. I laughed and said the brunette. I was interested, but wasn't sure I was going to pursue her. Mark told me he was going to set it up because he wanted the other young lady. Later that night, I received a call from Mark with her number.

I started talking to one of them, and she was beginning to like me as well. They would bake cookies for the team for our away games. After finding out my favorite cookie was the sugar cookie, I started getting my own bag with a dozen or so sugar cookies.

We talked for most of the season, and she was really good to me. Not only was I getting cookies, but if I needed any money, she would give me some. She bought me a nice polo for my birthday. I could use her car if I wanted. She was a down chick. However, when she told me how much she liked me, I started to put some distance between the two of us.

To be honest, I called her and told her I didn't think it was gonna work out between us. I could hear on the phone that I had hurt her. I laughed and moved on. It really didn't bother me that I was "heartless" to the girls I was with in high school.

At this point, basketball, girls, and money (whenever I could come up with some) were pretty much all I thought about. Unfortunately, it wasn't in that order. Basketball was last.

I was chasing girls either by myself or with my homeboys. I even found myself in the principal's office a couple of times because of an issue with a girl.

Once, when the bell rang for lunch to end, the police officer who often patrolled our school approached me. He asked if they could talk to me before class started. I told him that I needed to use the bathroom, and then I would go to the office.

I spent a minute in the restroom, trying to come up with something I did to make me go to the principal's office. Nothing came up, so after washing my hands, I went into the office.

The police officer, the dean, and the principal were all waiting for me. Not having a clue why I was in there, I was a little nervous at first. Then the officer told me that there was a problem they thought I could help with.

Two girls were about to fight over me, and they wanted me to step in before that happened.

With a big smile, I agreed to speak to the young ladies so we could resolve the issue.

They called the first girl down, and she was visibly upset. As soon as she came in the room, she started yelling at them to discipline me. She saw me and the other girl getting into my car yesterday, skipping school.

Now, before I continue, I want to explain this situation.

This girl, who is trying to get me in trouble for skipping school, is a girl that I'm seeing on the side. I have a girlfriend, and it's not her or the girl I skipped school with.

But in her defense, I did skip school the day prior, and I was with the young lady that she was talking about.

I didn't remember that they rode the same bus. So while I was outside waiting in my car for her to come out, like she was catching the bus, the other girl was on the bus that she was pretending to catch. She saw everything.

She started yelling about getting my girlfriend in the office to let her know I was skipping with this other girl. I said okay. I told her we could call my girlfriend down to see what she says, but why was it this girl's concern who I was with?

Things had started circulating about me and this other girl, though, so I told this girl it was in her best interest to keep quiet. Yelling in the principal's office wasn't the right time for this. So when we were asked if everything was okay, we both said yes.

While the girl troubles were new, the summer before my senior year wasn't much different when it came to my workout. I played some pickup ball, but I didn't do any individual work on my game. And it showed.

My game had dropped considerably from my sophomore year. However, I could still shoot, just not at as high a percentage. I could still dunk, but not all the fancy things I could do in my sophomore year. I really let life get in the way of the goal I had set for myself many years ago.

Since I had my car and didn't need to ask for money, I was out all the time—either chasing girls or just hanging out. I lost my focus.

In the first game of the season, I wasn't hitting the three (0-6); however, I finished with fifteen points and five rebounds.

The following Saturday, I shot better, hitting 8-17 from the field and 3-5 from the three-point line. I also had seven rebounds that game.

The following week, I played a better game, scoring twenty-one points and eleven rebounds. I shot only 3-9 from the three-point line, but I shot 7-16 overall from the field.

In my next game, I had twenty-two points and five rebounds. I even led all players in scoring that night.

After the first four games that year, the newspaper had me averaging 20.3 points, shooting 32-62 (.516) from the field and .769 from the free-throw line.

At the North-South game, I thought I would light them up like I did the year before. That's not how it worked out. That was one of my worst games to date. I only had two points, and I was 0-10 from the field and 0-4 from the three-point line. Only three rebounds, too.

I was determined to do better in the next game. Like another player on the other team, I got off to a good start.

The newspaper said, "Leading scorers Logan Wilkes of the Vikings and Bernie Madden of the Braves combined for 50 points, which was kind of a letdown, since they combined for 39 in the first half."

I ended the game with twenty-four points and five rebounds.

My next game was almost as bad as the 0-10 night against North. I was 3-12 and 0-6 from the three-point line.

Me chasing girls and not working out had finally caught up to me. I was up and down and not putting up back-to-back good games. I was very inconsistent.

I needed to work on it.

Chapter 6: One Bad Break

December 29, 1994. We had a morning practice around nine or ten a.m. We were preparing for the Wabash Valley Classic, a tournament held over Christmas break. In 1994, there were teams from Indiana, Kentucky, and Cincinnati. There were some good teams in this tournament.

I was having a good practice. My three-point shot was starting to fall again, and I had confidence in my game that I hadn't had in a long time. Practice was almost over, and we started to scrimmage with the junior varsity team. We went up and down the court a few times; things were going well.

When someone from the junior varsity got a steal, my eyes got big, and I was determined to send his shot to the moon! He saw me coming and faked. I jumped—then he undercut me. I tried to break my fall with my arm. My elbow locked up, and I broke both bones in my forearm. There was a snap that sounded like a chicken bone breaking. It happened so fast.

I tried to get up, and my arm just went limp. The JV coach told me to lie there. I told him, "I'll never play again."

Even though he told me not to talk like that, I knew it was the truth.

There was some commotion on the other side of the court. One of my boys was there, looking pissed. They had to hold him back, telling him the dude didn't do it on purpose. It didn't matter, though. The damage had been done.

As I lay on the court, I was in the most pain I had felt in my life. My arm started to bleed from the hole my bone put through my skin. My arm began to swell up, and it was only getting bigger the longer I lay there. The coaches called an ambulance.

Later that afternoon, I had a two-hour surgery. I remember feeling much better, but still in a lot of pain. The doctor came in that evening and told me I was going to have another surgery the next day or the day after.

I didn't think it was going to be a long surgery, so I was telling everyone to come see me an hour after the surgery.

I was only supposed to be in surgery for two hours, but I was in there for six. The doctor said he had to clean some red stuff off my bone, but he was unsure what it was. He later had someone check if paint was missing from the floor.

Not only was paint missing, but an eighth of an inch of the wood from the floor was also gone.

I ended up with a rod in one bone from the wrist to the elbow, and a plate with six screws in the other bone. I also lost motion in my arm. I was unable to lay my hand flat.

When I was released from the hospital, my father took me to the school so we could see the hole in the floor where my bone hit. I was given the game ball from the first game I missed. All my teammates signed it.

As I walked up the stairs to my house, I was shooting it in the air with my left hand, and I broke down and started to cry. I didn't know what I was going to do. I only ever wanted to go to college to play basketball. With how I'd done the last two years, what team was going to take a chance on me?

And because I was so focused on basketball, I didn't work hard on my grades. Just enough to pass — that was all I needed.

I decided to rehab every day and work hard to get my arm back to normal. I attended the home games and sat on the bench to cheer my teammates on. It hurt because all I wanted to do was play ball.

At first, I couldn't make the away games because of my arm. The doctor didn't want me to ride the bus, and then I lost interest in being there.

I can remember the sectionals that year. I was almost done with rehab. The doctor wouldn't let me play, but he did let me warm up with the team. I sat on the bench as we lost to Northview. I just wanted to get on the court one more time.

But it didn't happen that way.

That night, sitting on the bench with a healed arm and an aching heart, I realized that one break had changed everything. And for the first time, I had to figure out who I was when the game wasn't there to carry me.

Chapter 7: Me vs Me

Breaking my arm was the changing point of my life. I felt like life was over.

When I went back to school, I was mad at the world. I also witnessed something I didn't realize existed at the time. There was a teacher who always asked if I was going to dunk and if we were going to win the next game. I saw this same teacher walking toward me in the hall. He walked right by me, looked at me, and kept walking up the hall without saying a word.

I did feel like some of the teaching staff treated me different. I didn't get away with things like before. I didn't want to be there, and I acted like it. For the first time ever, I got suspended.

I was getting into trouble for little things, so the dean and principal decided they would let me into a program for seniors who had jobs, since I only needed two classes to graduate. I would go to school for three hours and then go to work. I quit my job soon after, so I would just go to school for three hours, then go home.

But I got bored and ended up going to school at lunch to hang out with my friends. The dean soon stopped me from coming back to the school. He told me that since they let me out early, I didn't need to come back.

I started to skip school altogether and hang out with some of the guys who sold drugs. Since I wasn't working, I thought about selling drugs myself.

I started by talking to a guy in my grade who was selling. He told me if I gave him one hundred dollars, he would sell the drugs and give me two hundred. After a week or so, I didn't get my two hundred dollars, and I asked him what was going on. He told me that I would have to sell the drugs myself and gave me my money back. I took that money and bought drugs for the first time.

At this time, crack cocaine was booming. There were many guys my age selling drugs and making a lot of money. They were buying cars, putting thousands of dollars in those cars to fix them up. Everything from the paint, speakers, and amplifiers, rims, tires, interior—anything else you could think of, they did it to their cars. They were traveling and doing things I wanted for myself, so I jumped in. How could I not?

I had an older cousin whom we will call Rick. He was one of the coolest people I knew. He had a nice car with loud speakers, and he would drive through our alley playing a certain song. When I was younger, I would come down the stairs and wait for him to come in. He would take me with him as he rode through the hood. He even took me with him as he cheated on his wife with other women.

When I was with him, I could do things my parents wouldn't let me do. When I was in the eighth grade, he got me a 40 oz of Old English. We rode around, and I got drunk for the first time. I told him I wasn't feeling well, and he asked if I had eaten. When I said no, he took me to KFC and bought me some chicken.

I was still feeling sick, so he took me home. I went to my room and lay down. My friends from junior high came by that night, and I told them I was drunk. They told me they could smell the alcohol on me and that I should eat some peanut butter to get the smell off. I did not know if that helped or not.

When my parents came home, they asked why I was in bed so early. I told them that I had some chicken and thought it made me sick.

They called me down from my room and knew something wasn't right. They made me tell them that I had been drinking. It went as well as you would think.

My uncle also took me out when I was fifteen, before I got my permit, and taught me how to drive. He definitely wasn't the best role model, but I loved being with him, running the streets, and experiencing the nightlife.

Before I began selling drugs, my cousin came by and sold me some of his stereo equipment. He would tell me he wanted me to have it and that he was giving me a good deal. I had no idea he was on drugs himself at the time. I really thought he wanted me to have it. And maybe he did—but he definitely would've sold it to someone else for more money.

After I purchased drugs for the first time, he came by to let me know we needed to talk. I wondered if he had heard what I'd started doing. After spending five to ten minutes talking to my mom and dad, he took me outside. I thought he was going to tell me not to sell drugs.

However, he told me he had asked the guy I purchased drugs from if I was selling, but the guy wouldn't tell him—he told him to ask me himself.

So Rick asked me if I was selling drugs, and I just smiled. Not knowing where this conversation was going, I told him yes.

He then told me that he would use from time to time.

I was in shock. Although I had my suspicions and I'd heard things in the streets, to hear it come out of his mouth was something else. He then asked me if I had any, and I told him yes.

He wanted me to sell to him, but I couldn't—because he was my cousin. I didn't want him using. But he brought up one point: if I didn't sell to him, he would just get them from someone else. He also told me he would never tell anyone where he bought from, so I wouldn't get in trouble.

That day wasn't the only time I sold him drugs. I knew what I was doing was wrong, but I did it anyway.

My outlook on life was different and ignorant, to say the least. If I could do it over, I would have never sold him drugs. To this day, I have regrets for what I did.

Being around the drug, I was able to see the effects it had on people. And to give it to a family member that I looked at like a big brother—that was one of the lowest things I've done in my life. I watched this drug tear apart his life.

However, at the time, he gave me what I thought was a good excuse to sell drugs to him, so I did.

He would let me come by his house and break my drugs down. He would also help me sell. I left the drugs at his house early in the evening and picked up my money later.

I wasn't making a lot of money—just two or three hundred dollars a week starting out. But I met some guys through him who were selling drugs and really seemed to know what they were doing.

As I continued to hang with guys who sold drugs, along with Rick, they taught me the game. I always thought I knew how to hustle, but this could have landed me in jail. So I stuck with the guys I thought were street smart and hadn't been in and out of jail. Most of them were older than me and had been hustling for a while.

I learned a lot from those older guys. I would sit and talk to them for hours. There were five older guys I would listen to and take advice from. On many occasions, they would let me ride with them, and when we saw someone "looking," they would let me serve them. One of the OGs would actually get the dope from me and serve it to the person buying it.

Because of these guys, I went from making two to three hundred dollars a week to five or six hundred a week. Most of my money was made on the weekends with my cousin Rick.

My time would mostly be spent with drug dealers on the weekend and my friends from junior high during the week. The only money I made through the week would be if Rick called, or from two or three other customers. However, I started to hit the streets more and learned that the people I served with the OGs remembered me and would always ask if I was "holding"—asking if I had any drugs on me to sell.

I didn't pick up a ball at all, and I didn't even watch much on television. I had lost all interest in basketball. The game that I loved more than anything got replaced with another game.

My mother and father didn't know what I was doing, but they had heard some of my friends were selling drugs. Both my mom and dad would say that there were only two things that happened to people selling drugs: death or jail. My father often talked to me about going to prison, because he had seen some of his family and friends go in and out of prison.

Although I didn't want to go to jail or die, I didn't care about what they said. All I wanted to do was hustle. This was my new love. I loved the whole process, not just making the money. The hustle took over my love for basketball.

I called a friend who also sold drugs one night to get a quarter ounce of crack. He said he was out but would have some soon. He never called back.

The next morning, he called for a ride to school. When I got there, he told me he had what I called for the night before. I didn't have enough time to put it up, so I took it to school with me. Having it sit in my car made me nervous, so I went to the nurse and told her I was sick. She called my grandmother, who gave permission to send me home—she was on my emergency card. (My grandma would always say, "Send him home," and she was my way out of school whenever I needed.)

I took the drugs to Rick's house. I broke it down and bagged it up. I hid the majority of it and took the rest to hit the street and make some money.

I continued to sell drugs after school was out. Somehow, I thought I would do it forever. It was very easy to sell because there were so many people using it. You could just ride down the street, see someone looking for crack, and sell it to them right out the window of the car.

Why would I stop?

Chapter 8: AK

Only a couple of months after school was out, I was driving down the street and saw an ambulance and police with their lights on. As I approached the intersection, I saw a Cadillac that looked like a guy who played on the basketball team with me. He was a good friend who would even come by my parents' house to cut my hair. He was also the guy who had my back when I thought Matt was going to attack me in practice.

He was a year older than me, but when he was a senior and I was a junior, he would often give me a ride home. We would work out sometime in the summer. He'd come and get me, and we would run hills with some other guys on the team.

I wanted to stop when I saw his car, but I had drugs on me and I was afraid to stop. So I went to Rick's house and chilled for a minute.

I wasn't there five minutes when I started to get phone calls asking me if I had heard what happened to that friend of mine. A good friend told me he had been shot in the head. Someone tried to rob him and shot him.

I called his phone, and his voicemail was full, but I could hear his voice one more time.

The shot to the head left him brain-dead, but his other organs were working, so he was on life support for a day or so, since he was an organ donor.

I went to the hospital the next morning to see him before they took him off life support. This was an eye-opening event for me because I had never lost a friend before.

Although I had mixed emotions about what I was doing, I must admit those mixed emotions got clearer. I kept selling drugs.

I wanted to stop. I wanted to leave it all alone. But I couldn't.

I really didn't care if the same thing happened to me. Don't get me wrong—I didn't want to die. But I really didn't care.

I went to my man's funeral, and as I saw him lying there, I couldn't help but think: *What if that was me?*

This was the first death of a friend of mine, but it wasn't the last.

Chapter 9: No Change

I got an opportunity to get a good job where my mother worked. I thought I would stop selling drugs since I got a decent job. However, I didn't stop—I just slowed down some. I enjoyed having the extra money on top of my check. There were other guys there who sold drugs, and there were people there who used drugs as well. I learned by talking to the right people who were okay to sell to and who weren't. I was soon selling to some of the people I worked with.

In September of 1996, only a year after I graduated, I had my first son. It was one of the best days of my life. I remember being at the hospital and seeing him for the first time. It was a joy that I hadn't felt before. I thought I would be able to stop selling drugs because I had a decent job, and I wanted to be here for him. However, months after he was born, I was laid off, so I started to sell drugs full-time.

One of my customers was a guy who worked with me. He had been there for a while, so he still had his job when I got laid off. I would give him more than he paid for, plus I would let him owe me until Friday, when he would get paid. His wife and their oldest son were also on drugs. I would meet them at their house about half an hour after they got off work to get my money from what I fronted them. I would also bring more drugs for them to buy. I knew what they made since I used to work there. They would give me most of their check, between what they owed me and what they would buy. I wonder how they paid bills if they were giving me most of their money.

By this time, I didn't have any compassion for too many people. All I cared about was getting my money, so that's what I did. I got my money and was on my way.

I can remember seeing my son one day at my girlfriend's house at the time. I had some speakers and an amplifier in my trunk   I hooked them up myself. Well, I had to unplug the amp when I was parked for a while and then plug it back in when I was leaving because it would drain my battery.

After visiting with my son, I opened my trunk, plugged my amp in, and took off. I had a gram of crack cocaine on me that I left in my car. Dangerous.

As I shut the trunk, I saw the police riding down the street. I had a funny feeling when I saw them, so I put the dope in my mouth and proceeded down the street. I turned the corner and had only gone about three or four blocks when I was pulled over. Once I saw the lights, I swallowed it.

This was something I had learned from one of the older dealers I associated with. I was told later that if that bag had been busted, I could have died.

When I stopped the car, there was a police car in front of me, two on the side, and one behind me. They asked me to step out of the car, and as soon as I stepped out, two cops with gloves on went into both of my front doors.

I thought they were going to drop something in my car and take me to jail. I was watching them go through my glovebox, and I looked up and saw two friends of mine—one of whom also sold drugs—

looking on. They looked at me and threw their hands up as if to ask what was going on. I shrugged my shoulders as if to say I didn't know.

Once they went through my car, they looked at the cop standing by me, and he shook his head no. The cop told me I was free to go.

I asked why I was pulled over, and he told me someone was involved in a shooting in the area, and the car involved was like mine.

This was the first time I had been afraid something bad was about to happen. However, after I was allowed to leave, I got myself together, and it was back to business.

I had an associate who was in the dope game. My cousin would work on his car from time to time, so I would see him around my cousin's house. He wasn't a good friend, but we saw each other often. He was older, and we would talk and joke around every time we saw each other. He was a real cool guy and was deeper into the game than I knew.

I can remember seeing him one day, and he wasn't the same. He wasn't talking the same, nor did he joke around like he used to. I thought he was acting different, but I didn't think too much of it and kept moving.

One day, we both pulled up at the gas station at the same time. He was so low in his seat, I didn't even notice him at first. I thought something wasn't right. I spoke to him, and he looked at me with a look I can't explain—but I won't forget.

Less than a week later, he was found shot multiple times, and left on the streets.

I don't know the whole story. However, I did run into his child's mother, and she told me she heard it was over drugs. She also confirmed there were people who had been looking for him for a few weeks, which explained why he was acting different and riding so low in the seat.

I mentioned a cousin (Rick) who knew what I was doing, so he would not only let me break down and bag up my drugs, but he would also help me sell the drugs from his house to people he knew who were on drugs. There were times I would just leave my stuff there and go back to pick my money up later that night.

I thought I had an airtight system because I didn't have to sell dope every day, and I was making good money. My name wasn't on the streets like many of the other guys I hung with.

One night, my cousin and I went to a spot they called the "jungle." It was a bootleg spot where they sold alcohol, and many people looking for drugs would be there. I sat in the car and listened to music or talked on my cell phone while my cousin was inside trying to sell the drugs for me. He would come out after selling some drugs, give me the money, and we would be on our way.

We went to this spot often—probably too often— since someone eventually told my father they saw my car there. This was the first time my parents heard anything about what I was doing.

My father had another long talk with me about selling drugs, and I knew I had a decision to make.

I knew that I could get some serious time for what I was doing, so I decided to switch my hustle. I left the crack alone, but I would get some "soft," or regular, cocaine, for a couple of females I knew who snorted it.

At the time, I convinced myself it was safer. I told myself it was different. But deep down, I knew I hadn't really changed—I just shifted the mask I was wearing.

Chapter 10: Time for Change

I was smoking weed every day, all day, and I thought if I sold weed, I could smoke for free—plus, I wouldn't get much time in jail if I were to get caught. At this time, there weren't a lot of people selling weed. I thought I'd jump in early and sew it up. Unfortunately, I didn't know too many people to sell weed to. I had some money saved up, so I didn't worry about not making much until my clientele grew.

I went to school with a guy who was selling pounds of weed and other drugs, so I got in contact with him and started buying two ounces at a time. That wasn't a lot, but I was going through it in about two days. I sold most of it and smoked the rest. I was going to his house every other day for a couple of weeks to get two ounces. I decided to move up to a quarter pound of weed, and I would go through that pretty quick as well. It was like the longer I sold weed, the more my clientele grew.

I would often visit this friend's house. One day, I was watching the news and saw that the police had busted him for marijuana and other drugs. I didn't think about the many times I had been to his house, or the police thinking that I went there for drugs. All I could think about was where I was going to get my weed from.

Luckily, I had a few people from whom I would get my weed at this time. I had another friend with whom I played junior high basketball who was selling marijuana, and I got some weed from him on multiple occasions.

I took him to get a pound one day, and after we got it, I was taking him to break it down. We saw one of the older guys, who gave me advice about the drug game, coming down the opposite side of the street. Back then, we would swerve at each other, just playing around. I wasn't aware there was a cop behind me. He was. He turned his lights on and pulled me over.

I gave him my license. He looked at it and asked, "Bernie, what are you doing now? Still playing ball?" I told him that I was looking for a job, no longer playing. He let me go and told me to be more careful.

There was another time when I went to get some weed from this same friend. There wasn't much weight around, so I was looking for something to smoke. I called my friend and he told me he would have some soon. When I went to his house, he had more than he was supposed to. I knew I had to get some, so I told him I'd get some money and be back.

When I returned to his house, I saw the K-9 unit truck parked on the corner. I didn't think much of it because he lived in the middle of the block, so I went through the alley and pulled in the back. I went to the door, and the police answered and asked me if I was there to buy drugs.

I said no.

I was asked to come inside, where I saw my friend and others handcuffed. They took my information (name, address, and telephone number). They walked me outside and asked if they could go through my car. I said yes. They looked in the windows with flashlights, but they never opened the doors or went through the car. I had some cigars and rolling papers in the seat. The officer asked if those were my rolling papers. I said yes. They looked at each other and told me I could go.

That didn't make me slow down. I just wanted to find someone with enough product so that I could expand my own business.

So, I found a couple of guys who were moving pounds of weed. I started to get weed from them. My clientele grew then. My smoking habit grew, too. I would wake up, smoke all day, and then sleep. I was moving probably a pound or two a week by this time. People would always ask for more, but I didn't have it. I couldn't purchase as much as they wanted and needed.

I was on the streets more than ever now, and my relationship with my son's mother suffered. When my first son was born, I was there. I was still trying to hustle, but I was low-key. I spent most of my time with her and my son. I would hustle when I could, but I was a boyfriend and father first.

Now, it was different. I could do whatever I wanted. I thought that because I was paying for everything, I was being the best father and boyfriend I could be. It was an obvious lie, and I knew it. I would be in strip clubs, talking crazy to women. I would be in the club buying drinks and trying to hook up with other women.

At this point, our relationship was off and on. I didn't understand how she could not want to be with me. I couldn't see the person I was becoming, but she obviously saw it.

During this period, I met the mother of my second son. I knew who she was, but I didn't have any way to get in contact with her. We both used to work at K-Mart when I was still in high school. I spoke to my friend and asked him to get the number for me, since they were about the same age and knew many of the same people.

We clicked right away. And to be honest, although neither would admit it, I think she's a lot like my mother, and that's why we clicked so well. She had her own place, and I would often stay over there. And as much as I thought I could settle down and do better, I was wrong.

I was turning into a monster. What I was doing to my first child's mother wasn't fair. However, I chose to play with someone else. Don't get me wrong—I loved my son's mother, both of them—but being the man I was at the time, I wasn't mature enough for a relationship.

I was making more money now, though. Everyone respected me.

I had the world in my hands.

Or so I thought.

Chapter 11: Two of a Kind

It was a Friday—payday—and business was good! If you know Terre Haute, then you're likely aware that there aren't many options for young adults to do. Besides the couple of small clubs, we would attend some campus parties just for something to do.

Earlier that day, my cousin Antonio called and asked if I'd heard about the campus party that Zay Mixx was DJing and if I wanted to go. I said sure and asked when he wanted to make an appearance. He laughed and said Eleven. Then we could put one in the air and grab a drink before we left.

I made some pickups and drop-offs before I got to Antonio's house. I had to. It was Friday, and while money moved through the week, Fridays and Saturdays were the biggest nights. I took the bulk of what I had to one of my spots, and then it was time to holla at Antonio.

As soon as I got there, we kicked back and put a few in the air. He poured a drink and handed me the bottle.

"Pour your own poison," Antonio told me.

Soon, we hopped in my Caddy and I drove to the party. Of course, we smoked a blunt on the way there. It wasn't far from Antonio's house, but it wasn't on campus either. However, it was a house party thrown by some college students. We arrived at the party, put the blunt out, and hopped out of the car.

You could hear the music playing from outside the house. As we approached the door, we saw a couple of guys collecting a few dollars per person. We paid and went in. We made our way back to where all the DJ equipment was set up, and that's where we spotted Zay Mixx. He looked up from a crate full of records, smiled, and threw his hand up.

All three of us talked for a minute before Antonio walked off, leaving us to talk a little more. Unfortunately, the music was too loud to let us talk as we wanted to, since we hadn't spoken in length in years. We exchanged numbers and agreed to keep in touch.

After giving Zay a pound and walking away, I spotted Antonio standing near a wall, talking to a female. I stopped, not wanting to interrupt his conversation. As I scanned the room, I saw a guy I'd known for a while, but we never really talked. However, I had heard from one of my people that he was the plug. He was the guy who could get me whatever I needed (weed). He was a very low-key person, and I really didn't think this was the place to approach him.

For whatever reason, I approached him anyway.

I started out with some small talk, mostly sports, as I tried to find a way to ask for some type of business relationship. Still trying to put my words together, he looked at me and told me I needed to call him sometime. We both knew what he meant.

As we exchanged numbers, Antonio walked up, and the three of us spoke for a little bit before Antonio and I left the party.

This was a memorable night for me. I got reacquainted with my cousin and met THE PLUG.

Before this night, I was just a young hustler trying to make enough money to have fun, be able to spend a couple of hundred here and there, have a few grand saved up, and be able to smoke as much as I wanted. I really didn't see the big picture.

These two guys really helped me see life very differently. On the one hand, you had a guy who was working a 9–5 and DJing on the side as a hustle. On the other hand, there was a very successful hustler.

First, my cousin Antonio. He worked at a factory for years and was also an accomplished DJ. A little older than me, he was successful, and people didn't even know how successful he actually was as a DJ. He wasn't the type of guy to brag about his accomplishments. However, he had a list of them.

After getting his number at the party, we talked on multiple occasions. We would have lunch on occasion, and he would give me some advice. He was always thinking two steps ahead and tried to get me to do the same. He knew what I was doing and never said I shouldn't do it, but he would always talk about doing legitimate business.

Some of my future legitimate businesses were his ideas. I even started DJing myself. My comedy show was also his idea. I spent some money on equipment, and Zay taught me a few things on the ones and twos.

I really enjoyed being around Zay. He treated me like a little brother.

We would often take trips to Chicago to look for rare albums. In the car on the way to Chicago, I would usually pick his brain, and he would offer advice as well. We became very close during this time. I looked at him as a big brother.

On a trip to Chicago to find some vinyl, he took me to a man who goes by the name of Juice. Now, for everyone who knows hip-hop, this is the only person to beat Eminem in a rap battle right before he became famous. This dude was incredible when it came to freestyling. He did a little something to the beat of the NFL song they used to play before commercials. We kicked it there for a while and discussed music along with some current events.

I was able to meet many "famous" people through DJ Zay. Although he was a good influence on me, taught me a lot, and I wanted something legal, I was still looking to move up in my illegal business.

To do that, I called up the other person I talked to at the party. When I called, he already knew what I wanted. I found out later that he had heard I was trying to do my thing with the weed, just like I had heard he was the man.

"How much are you moving?" he asked.

"A couple of pounds a week," I said.

"How much do you need?"

"I can pay for one. Let's move from there."

He came by one of my spots to drop it off. I sat in the car, and we talked before the transaction. He was telling me he had wanted to work with me. I could move so much more if I had a consistent connect. I agreed.

He proceeded to let me know he was that guy. Whatever I wanted, he would have—and could even give me some on consignment, so I wouldn't have to come out of my own pocket. It sounded good, so I got the pound I came for and left.

I called back a few days later to get another one, and we started to discuss the price. At this point, I was tripping because we hadn't done a lot of business, and this guy was already willing to give me this product at a price lower than I'd ever seen.

He said he wanted to help me get on for real and make some real money. I didn't know why he wanted to look out for me.

"I like the way you think, but you ask a lot of questions."

"Let's get it," I said, smiling.

This guy had whatever I needed. My clientele grew even more because of him. I was up to at least five to ten pounds a week now, and things were going well. I would buy some and get some fronted to me, and that's when the money really started to come in.

When he first told me about fronting me some weed, I was against it, though. All the hustlers I was around told me never to take more than I could pay for. Well, this man wanted to put me on way more than I could pay for. I knew I could move the weed—I just didn't want to be responsible for thousands of dollars if something went wrong.

However, after taking a pound here and a pound there on consignment, we discussed bigger numbers and how much I would have to put down on it. At this point, I would guess he brought anywhere from fifty to one hundred pounds a month. To my knowledge, he was one of two people who brought weed into the city in those amounts.

The difference was—my man kept weed. He would often re-up before he ran out, so he could keep things flowing.

By this time, we had developed a very strong business and personal relationship. He would give me whatever I asked for on consignment. When I say whatever I want, I mean whatever. I was given fifty pounds at a time on multiple occasions and didn't have to give him a penny when I received the weed.

One reason I believe we had such a good relationship is that if I owed him money, he would get it when I told him he would get it. He also knew I would go into my own pocket if there was an issue with his money.

Living in Terre Haute, there weren't a lot of places to shop. When you were making as much money as us, you wanted to spend it. We would go to Chicago and spend thousands on one trip.

We didn't shop at the malls—we went to a couple of places where some celebs often shopped. When we walked in, you could see pictures of the workers with Snoop and other rappers, actors, and entertainers. I saw the iceberg gear and other things that rappers would rap about in songs.

The price tags left me dumbfounded. Remember—I come from Terre Haute. There wasn't a store that sold a (jean) jacket for $450 and matching pants for $150.

My man was doing his thing, joking around with some of the employees while he waited for them to bring him a few pairs of shoes to choose from. I, on the other hand, was contemplating buying these $150 jeans and $450 jacket (I did buy them both). If my memory serves me correctly, I brought about $2,500 with me. I probably spent about two thousand that day, and I didn't come home with a lot of bags. Everything was more expensive than I expected, but I was able to purchase some very nice things. He lived a luxurious lifestyle, and he wanted me to do the same.

I got a call from my man telling me he was out of town, but when he got back, he had something to show me. It was about a week later when we got a chance to get together. He came by my house early one afternoon. Eager to find out what this guy brought, I asked what he scored. He opened his Mitchell and Ness throwback jacket and showed off a $100,000 chain. He took it off and handed it to me.

As I'm examining the chain, wondering how long before I can get one, he pulls out an envelope with two or three papers in it. He handed me one of the papers that came from another jeweler, where he took the chain to get it appraised. I knew I had to make plans to see that jeweler when I was comfortable spending that kind of money.

I remember being in Chicago one Saturday morning when he got a call from a young lady asking if or when he was going to see her while he was in town. He asked me if I minded picking her up so she could kick it with us for a couple of hours, since he hadn't seen her in a while. Now, this wasn't his girlfriend or anything like that. He had a very attractive woman at home. But I said it was fine.

We picked her up from her house. She got in and was very excited to see my man. We went to the mall, and I picked up a throwback jersey and some shoes, but my man didn't buy anything. He did pick up a pair of boots for a young woman he didn't see more than five times a year, though.

We pulled up to drop her off, and she asked if we wanted to go to the movies later with her and her best friend. My man looked at me and smiled, asking what I thought. Of course, I said sure.

We left to get something to eat. As stated before, we were going to an early movie for some reason, so we didn't go far from where we were. After eating, we picked up his young lady friend and headed over to get her friend, who didn't live too far from where we were.

We pulled up to the house, and this beautiful young lady came out. It was almost like slow motion as I watched her come toward the car. She got in, and we all got introduced.

We started some small talk before the movie, and we were feeling each other. She was a little younger than me—eighteen or nineteen, if my mind serves me right. After the movies, we exchanged numbers before dropping them both off and heading to our hotel. I wanted to keep in contact with her, but I didn't. Out of sight, out of mind. And now, without the ladies, we could discuss business.

He would often try to get me to quit smoking weed. I asked him if he ever smoked. He said yes, but now it was just about the money. I could definitely understand what he was saying, but I was making more money than I knew possible off of weed.

"Do you have anything to smoke?" he asked.

"Not at all."

"Do you want to smoke?"

"Yes!"

"If my man is available, I'll smoke with you."

He made a phone call, telling the dude on the other end that he would be right over. Come to find out, he had a homeboy who was doing his thing with high-quality weed.

We arrived at his condo. My man looked at me and told me, "This is a quarter-million-dollar condo." It was nice. Not real flashy or over the top, but you could tell whoever lived here had some money.

This guy named Jesse came out of a room as we made our way to the living room. He greeted my man like a long-lost brother. I was introduced as a cousin to my man. Dude showed me some love, and we all sat down.

After about an hour or so of small talk and the two of them telling a couple of stories, my man asked how much for a smoke sack. Jesse looked at my man with a straight face and told him his money was no good there. They both smiled as Jesse walked into another room and came out with a small bag of bright green weed. My man looked at it and handed it to me. I took a look and smelled the bag. With a big smile, I gave it back. It was starting to get late, so we left after some more small talk.

As we left Jesse's place, my man asked if I had something to roll the weed in. I didn't, but I asked him to stop so I could get a cigar. We approached a gas station a couple of blocks away. I hopped out and got a couple of cigars. Once I got back in the car, my man handed me the weed so I could roll up. I hadn't smoked all day, so I was ready. It took about a minute to break the weed down and roll the blunt. Once we got to the hotel, we smoked in the car. It was easily the best weed I had ever smoked up to that point.

While my smoking habit was pretty bad, I was making so much money that I didn't see a point in stopping. I wasn't an addict or dependent. If I needed to get clean, I wouldn't need to go to rehab or anything like that. I was around a lot of hustlers, though. This guy was probably the main reason I never went to prison. He thought of everything. When we went out of town to score, he would check the weather. We would go a day earlier or later if there was rain in the forecast. We would also dress down—old clothes, usually sweats and t-shirts. He never went over the speed limit. He was very patient. He wasn't greedy. There were times we could have scored, but if something didn't seem right, my man would cancel the transaction, and we wouldn't score from that person, even if I wanted to. He made sure everything was on point before making a move, and I learned to do that myself (for the most part).

This was one of the craziest times of my life. Not only was it crazy how fast the money was coming, but the things I experienced were also wild. When we got to the spot, we would meet a middleman. He would then call the man with the product. We would wait for him—or them—to bring it, and then we were on our way. We bought so much we couldn't even see if it was all there, and many times, they had the weed in different-size bricks—up to ten pounds per brick—so we'd have to wait until we got back to check. If it wasn't all there, we'd get the rest on the next trip. But while we waited, they would sit in the car, counting the money, and wouldn't let us leave until they had counted a certain amount.

My man had multiple connections, but there was one dude he went through regularly who really meant business. My man was NEVER short with the money, and he dealt with this guy all the time. While we were waiting for the transaction, his boys would be in a noticeable vehicle circling the block. The middleman told us they had guns and were there just in case anything didn't go right.

It was a dull purple van. These weren't like the people back home. These men would kill if the money weren't right. They were also robbing guys coming into the city to purchase. At the time, I didn't realize the kind of people I was dealing with. It didn't matter who was more involved—if something went down, I was just as guilty. I didn't even think about it then, as I put myself in more and more of these situations.

On the way up there, we had to be careful, since we were usually riding with over fifty thousand dollars. If we got caught, we'd lose all that money and couldn't provide any proof of how we earned it, which would probably lead to a tax evasion charge. On the way home, we'd be riding with huge television boxes, duffel bags, or whatever we could use to fit at least one hundred pounds of weed. On one occasion, we couldn't fit it all in the trunk—we had to put one in the back seat. My man had some extra air freshener, but it only helped for about the first half hour. By the time we were halfway home, the whole car smelled like weed.

And yet, we kept going. The risk, the money, the illusion of control—it all fed the fire. But deep down, even then, I knew I was walking a road that had only two endings. And neither of them led to peace.

Chapter 12: Who Does That?

I was on the streets more than ever now, and my relationship with my first son's mother suffered. It was no fault of her own. I had to be in the streets (or so I thought), and because I had money, I was blinded by it and all the things that came with it. We were off and on by this point, and during the period we weren't together, that was when I met my second son's mother.

I can remember the day my second son was born, July 24, 1999, for a couple of reasons. First, it was a special day for me because I was having another son. The second reason is that I went out of town to score some weed the morning before. That trip had to go right so I could be back in time to see my son being born. I went with my man, and we had everything planned so we could make it back in time for the birth of my son. This was the only time I was nervous on a trip to score weed.

We left early in the morning. When we got there, we had to wait. I didn't think I would make it back in time. However, we scored.

When we got back, I had to rush to the hospital; my son was less than an hour from being born. Later, I learned that her family was wondering why I was late, and why I was dressed that way. When I think back, I can't believe I would make a choice like that. The streets had consumed me by this time, and it really felt like a job to me.

I have to be honest. For the first time ever, I was respected by everyone. Before, I got love for being a decent basketball player. Notice I said decent. I didn't even get the respect I thought I deserved from basketball. But this game I was playing was different. When the money arrived, respect followed. If I had over fifty pounds at a time, the other hustlers respected me. When I was hanging with my man, I was hanging out around people with two, three, maybe five or ten times my wealth. It didn't matter. They still respected me. It's funny how I went from just a dude who could ball a little to a dude who was ballin'.

My boys were my life, though, and I was able to provide very well for them. I would go to Indianapolis and spend anywhere between $300 and $600 on clothes for them every time I went. Or five hundred in Chicago out of nowhere, so they could have something no other kid had. They didn't wear anything but name-brand clothes and the newest Jordans. I would spend time with my boys, and they would spend time together. I didn't want them ever to think I loved one more than the other. I wanted them to be like one hundred percent brothers, not half-brothers.

Although I would spend a lot of time with my boys during the day, I would spend all night hanging out, drinking, and smoking with my friends. I was a fixture in the small clubs we had. And because I had more weed than ever, I would smoke with everyone who was around. My homeboys didn't have to bring weed because I was always smoking. They would, however, bring some smoke, and I would match everyone who was with us.

I thought there was no way life couldn't get any better. I had plenty of weed to sell, and I could smoke all day. I had a team that was doing well, and I still had customers of my own. I was at the height of my career.

But sometimes, when you're standing on top of the mountain, you forget how far down the fall can be. And in the back of my mind, a quiet voice kept asking the one question I never dared to answer: *How long could this really last?*

Chapter 13: The Good Life

I was smoking with a friend who plays golf. He was convincing me to play, saying how much fun it was. I agreed, and one morning we were out on the golf course. It was fun, and as an added bonus, we could smoke if no one was around.

I kept getting calls from people that morning, telling me they had money for me and needed more weed. After finishing a round of golf, I went and picked up thousands of dollars. Not a bad morning.

That wasn't a one-time thing. There were times I would get a call in the late morning or afternoon to sell pounds. I would go and sometimes drink a beer or two, smoke for an hour or so, play video games, and then pick up a couple thousand dollars and be on my way.

The money was flowing, and I was working less than I ever had. My team was strong and moving the weed I fronted them. At this time, I wouldn't spend the change or dollar bills that I got from my purchases. I would have a shoebox full of one-dollar bills. At times, I would have over $700 in the shoebox, consisting of one-dollar bills.

The first weekend in May was one of my favorite times of the year. Those into horses or horse betting might have guessed the Kentucky Derby. Yes! The Kentucky Derby.

Now, it had nothing to do with the horses—in fact, out of the five-plus years I'd been to the Derby, I'd only been to Churchill Downs once. And we didn't go inside the track that day. The Kentucky Derby weekend, for those who have ever been, knows it's one big party! Many have said it was like the Freaknik that used to take place in Atlanta.

In the weeks leading up to the Derby, I had to find some clothes. I could go to the closet. I had a nice collection of Mitchell and Ness throwbacks—the Moon, Elway, George, and Malone (to name a few)—but my favorite and most expensive option was the Jackie Robinson jersey, which they only used for late games. It was $375, plus tax.

I had only worn the Jackie once and really wanted to put it on, but I decided to hit the mall in Indianapolis instead. That's where I found the Wilt Chamberlain purple and gold jersey. I also grabbed a pair of shorts and a couple of pairs of jeans for the trip. I didn't have any shoes to go with the Chamberlain, so I went into a couple of shoe stores before I spotted a pair of old-school Magic Johnson shoes—they weren't even one hundred bucks.

Needless to say, I left the mall with a few bags and my gear for the Derby. The only thing left to get would be some liquor and Backwoods cigars. Of course, I had the weed and a pocket full of money, so I was ready to hit the road.

Antonio wasn't going that year, and I would have been by myself if my man Darin hadn't ridden with me.

Pulling up to Darin's house, I popped the trunk for his bag and then took shotgun so he could drive. We hadn't hit I-41 yet, and we were already drinking Belvedere with pineapple juice and smoking a blunt.

Before we had left his driveway, though, he agreed to pick up my little brother from Vincennes University. He didn't answer, but we still headed that way.

Vincennes is only forty-five minutes from Terre Haute, so after rolling another blunt or two and answering a few phone calls, I didn't even call my little brother back until we got there. He still didn't answer.

Once we were on the campus, we found the main administrative building and got a room number. Even though I dropped him off one other time, I couldn't remember the room number. By the time we got to his room, he had just finished class.

I asked him if he wanted to go to the Kentucky Derby with us. Of course, he did, so he started getting his stuff together. He was a Kobe fan and had his jersey, along with a Michael Finley jersey, pinned to his wall. He very carefully removed the pins holding the Finley jersey first, folding it and placing it in his bag. He then, even more carefully, took down the Kobe jersey, holding it in the air and mumbling something about him being the greatest, and placed it in his bag.

This was pure entertainment. I told him he would have to drive, and I would take care of everything else. He agreed as he continued to gather his things, and then we hit the highway.

Darin and I were smoking and drinking. My little bro Sammy didn't smoke, and I wouldn't let him drink until later that night when he wasn't driving.

This year, we didn't get a room in Louisville. Since we waited so late to book the room, there weren't any available, so we stayed in Jeffersonville instead. We were only a few minutes away from the action.

When we got to the hotel, Sammy grabbed a luggage cart. We put our suitcases and any loose bags on, and then two $55 Belvedere vodka bottles on top. Sammy started pushing the cart toward the hotel—one of the bottles fell, smashing into a million pieces.

Darin looked at me, and we just started laughing, while Sammy turned around with a shocked look on his face, trying to apologize for dropping the bottle. Darin and I laughed harder. Just watching the bottle hit the ground was funny—probably because we had been smoking the whole way there. We also had a few mixed drinks to go with the weed. The laughter could have come from the fact that we didn't care. I mean, I could have bought five more bottles if I wanted to.

I may sound cocky, but I really wasn't. Or at least, I didn't think so. Why trip over it? It was only sixty bucks. I planned on "stunting" with the rest of them. Throw money around like they do.

It was time to hit a spot or two. After dropping the bags off in the room, rolling a pack of Backwoods, and making another drink for the road, we headed out to hit Broadway. Being that we stayed in Jeff instead of Louisville, we had to drive about five miles to get into Louisville.

Normally, the first place I would stop was my grandmother's house. I always tried to stop by to see her first whenever I was in town. This time it was different. We went straight for Broadway. I came here often, either for the Derby, visiting family, or the casino nearby, so I was the navigator.

Once we got close to Broadway, we all smiled like kids in a candy store.

There were so many people here that traffic on Broadway was basically stopped. People were getting in and out of their cars, standing in the middle of the street. Everyone was stunting and trying to show out. Music as loud as it could be. Women danced to the music while men videotaped their every move.

Here's where you would see it all. The throwback jerseys you couldn't find in the store—someone probably had them on. That perfect woman, or the one with the huge booty, or big breasts. Whatever you liked was there on Broadway.

We crept up Broadway, still smoking blunt after blunt. The police were out, so our first thought was to ditch the weed. But after looking around and seeing— and smelling—the weed smoke everywhere, I guess they just gave us a pass for smoking.

High as a kite, I was ready to holla at something. There were women everywhere! We would yell at damn near every woman we saw. After striking out a couple times, we got some numbers, but called others bitches because they wouldn't yell their numbers across Broadway or walk over to us.

Still smoking and feeling great, I was starting to get hungry. We were only about two or three blocks from King's Chicken. We got there, placed our orders, and then Darin asked if one of the women I met last year had any friends. I laughed and said I would give her a call. She was expecting me to call since we kept in touch and she knew I would be there for the Derby.

While on the phone, our food was ready, so we picked it up and headed back to the hotel. She agreed to meet us at the hotel with her friends so we could all have a drink or two before they went out for the night.

Still in the clothes we got there in, I wanted to go to the mall and see if I could find something rare, either for Sunday or just to add to my collection. So we hit Broadway one more time and headed to the mall. My little brother may have had only seventeen dollars in his pocket, so when we got inside, I slid him a few twenties. I told him I would still buy his food, but wanted him to have some spending money. Usually, I find something to purchase, but not this time.

We decided to return to the hotel, change our clothes, and get ready for the night. We got there and took turns showering. Sammy was getting changed and pulled out his Kobe jersey. He had been waiting to wear this jersey since we got there. I was already dressed and looking through the jerseys I brought. Pulling out the John Elway, I handed it to him. Nothing against Kobe, but it was a regular sixty-five-dollar jersey. The Elway was three hundred—and a throwback, like we were wearing. He was excited and ready to get the party started, asking if the women were going to show up. I told him they were on the way.

I spoke to her before calling DJ Zay. He was DJing celebrity parties and told me he could get me in, but there was a dress code. I didn't bring anything to get into a club like that. I could've bought something, but really, I didn't want to do the club thing. I wanted to hang out on the streets, to be on Broadway with whoever was out there. It was a different crowd. Zay once did a party where Michael Jordan was at after the Derby and could have got me in, but once again, I was on Broadway.

Twenty to thirty minutes later, there was a knock on the door. Sammy answered, and three young women walked in. We were still drinking when they got there. We ordered them drinks and let them "pour their own poison," like my man Antonio would say. After some small talk, joking around, and a drink or two, they left to go to the club. We had a decent time and said we would hook back up later. However, that wasn't the game plan.

My uncle once told me, "Nephew, you don't take sand to the beach." Broadway was the beach, and we were on our way.

Once we got there, it was more of the same thing. We hung out on Broadway for a while before calling it a night.

The next day, I had to see my grandmother since I hadn't seen her yet. As soon as we got there, she offered to feed us and asked if I needed anything. I was good and wanted to do for her, but the last time I tried to buy groceries, she slid the money into my jacket pocket. I enjoyed spending time with her, though, because I didn't see her very often.

Once we left, we started drinking and smoking as we made our way to a strip club. Sammy hadn't been to a strip club before—he was only nineteen. However, Louisville had a strip club where you could get in at eighteen. They didn't serve alcohol, though.

Even though I was having fun watching Sammy enjoy himself, I wasn't my usual self. I paid for a couple of dances for him, and we left. This day was no different from the night before. More time spent on Broadway, drinking, smoking, and just hanging out.

We checked out the next morning and headed home.

Chapter 14: Slow Down

It was the year 2000, and I was thriving. I was achieving great success. Finances were solid, my family was doing well, and my team was performing exceptionally. This may sound arrogant, but I was just a confident young man pursuing my goals.

Since I had it all, I decided to get away to see my homeboy (Marcus) in Chicago. We went to junior high and high school together. He was from Indiana, but after college, he stayed in Chicago, so he had some familiarity with the city.

Chicago was around a three-hour drive, so I made sure to get really high before hitting the road. I should mention that Marcus was going to help me out when I arrived, and I preferred not to drive without some potential advantage. After I landed, we made a quick stop to get prepared before heading out to the Sky Box.

Now this place had it all. I didn't know whether to call it a strip club or Dave & Busters. There was so much to play with, one could get lost in the ambiance. You name it, they had it. It was like the OJ Simpson defense team of fantasies. Needless to say, it was the best. I don't want to beat a dead horse, but this place had an all-star cast of strippers. All I kept thinking to myself was, I have to get up here more often.

One dancer came, then another, then another. Every time I came back from the VIP room, my man Marcus had another one waiting for me. I took her back to the VIP room. By then, he had two. I can't recall if they were kissing, but I definitely wanted it to last forever.

After rapping with girl after girl—sometimes two at a time—I came back to the table and finished my drink. I was feeling good about my decision to get away for a few days. I mean, the women were friendly, green is loud, and I still had money that I brought just to blow. It was getting late, and we decided to check out another spot before hitting up Harrold's Chicken and calling it a night. After a night of drinking, Harrold's was the perfect nightcap to a perfect night.

Marcus had to work the next morning, so he was up and at it early. While he was at work, I needed to find something to get into. So, I got myself together, rolled a couple for the road, and headed for downtown. Money had been very good to me lately, so in my mind, I had no limits!

You might spot me in stores such as Prada and La Perla. The new me actually went to shop, not just browse. There was a fair chance I ended up picking up a few items during my outing.

These moments to myself always had me reflecting on my lifestyle. Although I was a "drug dealer" and probably came off as one, the weed smell I brought around with me didn't bother me at this point. I was very proud of myself.

While driving around downtown Chicago alone (and smoking), I decided to check in back home to make sure everything was good. Before I could make a call, my friend Adam called and told me it'd been a great weekend and he had people waiting. I could hear the excitement in his voice.

He had plenty before I left, and he sold that and could move another five this weekend. He kept asking, "When are you coming home?"

I told him I wasn't certain and asked him to wait a moment and I'll call him back. I also checked in with my team members and found similar outcomes. Most are out or nearly out. Some I had fronted while others were paid in cash.

But at this time, I had at least ten thousand worth of weed that I fronted before I left and some more opportunities with Adam, so I decided to go back home the next morning. I explained the situation to Marcus when he got off work, and he told me we needed to hit a spot or two tonight.

Of course, I was going out, but to be honest, all I could think about was how much I had waiting for me, plus the money I could make. We went to one more club, had a beer, before I told him I was ready to go. I knew I had a long drive and wanted to be halfway rested before hitting the road in the morning.

Now, I usually got high as hell before hitting the road instead of carrying the weed with me. At least, that's what I did on the way up there, and it worked out fine. Against my better judgment, I decided to roll something for the journey.

It's funny what happens when you aren't focused. The money and potential gain at home blinded me. Not only did I smoke that blunt on the way home, but I didn't even think to get something to get rid of the weed smell. All I could think about was how fast I could get back home to get this money.

I had a good amount of gas, and my phone wouldn't stop ringing, so I was now going 85 in a 55 zone. I had traveled this highway many times, and I really knew better than to speed. Well, I was keeping an eye out, but it was too late now... In the rearview, I saw the red and blue flashing lights.

Even though I told Marcus I would return shortly for a visit, I decided to take the ten grams of weed home with me. The bag was in my pocket, and as I began to pull the car over, I attempted to push the bag into my boot. However, I wasn't able to get the bag fully down into my boot.

He asked for my license and registration. I thought maybe the weed smell was gone or not very strong, and for some reason, he wasn't going to say anything. After he gave me my license back, he told me everything was good with my license, but he smelled marijuana and wanted to know if I had been smoking.

I told him I smoked a blunt on my way home from Chicago. He told me to step out of the car. As expected, he found the ten grams in my boot, so he handcuffed me and put me in the back of his SUV.

He asked if I had any money on me. I only had two or three hundred in my pocket. And because of the good time I had at the Sky Box, and the clothes and gifts I bought, I only had a thousand in my suitcase. I told him I had a thousand dollars in my suitcase as well. He told me that it should be enough to bond out.

He then asked where the suitcase was. I told him it was in the trunk. He took my keys, opened my trunk, and got the money out for me. He walked back to the car and put the money in my pocket. I watched all this with my hands cuffed behind my back.

This was my first (and only) time with my hands handcuffed behind my back. As I rode to the police station, I thought about my future and what I would do once I got home.

I always thought that once I got arrested, I would stop selling drugs. To be honest, the thought of quitting barely crossed my mind. If it did, it was a quick thought that was dismissed when I thought about the money waiting for me back home.

I knew it was just a possession charge, and I could bond out, so it would just delay my arrival time. I had to play this "game" to get home so it could be business as usual. So, to set my game, I started some small talk with the arresting officer on the way to the station.

I asked him if he knew what my bond would be. He told me that they were taking my car to the car shop down the street to see if I had more drugs hidden in the car. They would remove my seats and search every inch of the car.

I paused. I had made so many trips on that same highway with, well, let's just say more to hide. I cleared that thought.

"How long do you think it will take to process me?"

"Not long if we don't find anything in your car," he laughed.

I laughed inside, knowing they wouldn't find anything. There was nothing to find. I had a feeling this guy thought I had more weed or that I was a dealer.

I have to be honest, I was clean. Everything on me was brand-new and of a brand name. I only mention that because it was brought up during my processing. They took my shoes and belt when I first got there, along with everything in my pockets. They saw the money and asked where I was coming from and where all the money came from. This was pocket change to me, and besides, anyone could have twelve hundred dollars. That's what I thought but didn't say.

I must admit, I was taken aback. I told them my parents gave me the money. They said I looked nice and asked what I did. I told them I was unemployed. Then she said my parents must have bought my clothes. I thought it was a joke and looked around. I was in a town I was told was prejudiced, and there was only one other Black man in there, behind bars.

I decided to play it cool and get out of there. They told me the charge and that bond was eleven hundred. I paid the money and, after about another hour, I was on my way back home—doing the speed limit, of course.

I couldn't be excited, though. I knew I would have to return to court and hire a lawyer.

I did pick up my money, and it was still business as usual. I visited my lawyer before attending court. He told me I could get probation since I hadn't been in trouble before. I went to court, and I was put on probation and given a probation officer. I could get it expunged from my record if I stayed out of trouble.

Although I had never been on probation, I knew plenty of people who were or had been on it, so going in to see my probation officer wasn't a big deal. The biggest concern I had was not being able to smoke, since I'd have to take a drug test at least once a month.

That's what I thought, anyway.

I traveled to meet my PO for the first time. Arriving early, I waited for about half an hour before speaking with him. When he called my name, I stood up as he beckoned me to walk back into his office.

He instructed me to take a seat while he removed his glasses and set them on the table, either out of frustration or fatigue. Regardless, I leaned back in my chair as he started explaining how this probation process would unfold. It seemed like a speech he had delivered countless times before.

In that conversation, he told me I would lose my license for six months. I would also have to come see him once a month and give a urine screen every time I came. I reminded him that I lived an hour and a half away. He told me I wouldn't have to come in. Instead, I could fax a paper once a month.

He did remind me that since I'm on probation, they could come into my home at any time. If I did what I was supposed to do and he didn't hear about me from other people, I wouldn't hear from him.

It sounded good to me, so I stood up, shook his hand, and headed out the door.

I had a nice drive home to think about my next moves. Being on probation put a little wrinkle in my plans. I didn't have a license now. (The probation officer did agree to let me drive to class, so I signed up for some college courses.) Although I didn't keep a lot of weed or money where I slept, I needed a new spot.

I got an apartment with Darin out in the country. I bought new furniture, bedroom items, and other essentials for the place. That cost me about $3,000. Since I lost my license for six months, I bought a new 49cc scooter for $1,700.

I was going to spend a lot of time at home, so I needed something to keep me occupied. I spent another five thousand dollars on some DJ equipment. My lawyer was thirty-five hundred dollars. I thought about giving up selling weed until my probation was over. However, I was spending so much money, I knew I had to keep moving the pounds.

The first six months were business as usual. I was faxing a paper to my probation officer every month, and I hadn't been called to drop a urine screen, so I was smoking every day, all day. I'd also been driving like I had a license once I got enrolled in school.

My probation was so lax that it got to the point where I bagged up about fifty pounds a couple of times at my apartment.

About seven months into my lease, everything changed.

My man Adam called me one morning, saying he had something to share. I wasn't sure what had happened, but all I remember is him saying he was short on the money he owed me. I paused for a moment. That wasn't like him.

I asked him how short he was. He said he didn't have any of it.

I hung up the phone feeling incredulous. While I was frustrated about the four thousand dollars, it's important to realize that this young man likely generated around a hundred thousand dollars for me during our business dealings. So, what truly troubled me was the thought that the cash flow would begin to slow down.

I had another guy who would sell about what Adam sold, but he wasn't as loyal. He would deal with a couple of other guys for whatever reason. At the time, I was only dealing with him occasionally. The other big customers I had were also falling off.

I wasn't all the way out, though. I was still making money. However, it wasn't flowing as before.

There were some cocaine dealers who switched their hustle to weed. We didn't hold the same market share as we once did.

And just like that, the game started shifting—and I knew I had to shift with it or get swallowed whole.

Chapter 15: Real Change

Not only was the game changing, but so was my life. My boys were getting older, and I was really enjoying the time I spent with them. I signed my oldest son up to play ball at the Boys Club. I had him shooting on the Nerf goal he had in his room. He loved to play, and I enjoyed teaching him.

I decided this was the best time for me to leave the game for good. I didn't think this day would come so soon. Just six months ago, I would have said I'd hustle forever. But the next conversation I had with my man was me telling him I was out. I decided to get a job and raise my sons.

Since I was taking classes at Ivy Tech, I met a woman who was impressed with me. She thought I was smart and had a lot of potential. She asked me to attend some programs they had at the school, and if I did, she would help me get a job. I was actually just about finished with one of the programs when she got me an interview at PolyOne, a factory that produced plastic pellets. It was a very dirty job, but I was starting out at fifteen to sixteen dollars an hour.

I couldn't tell Mrs. James that I smoked weed and didn't know if I could pass the urine screening. Some people would take someone else's urine and pass it off as their own, but I couldn't do that. I decided to quit smoking and clean myself out so I could pass the urine screen with my own urine.

I asked some veteran smokers what I should do to get it out of my system as soon as possible. I was given many remedies—everything from drinking bleach to buying a cleaner to "flush you out" within two to four hours.

I was often told I had a weed problem since I smoked so much. I didn't think I had a problem because I always said I could quit if I wanted to. The first week or two was tough, though. I was sweating all the toxins out of my body, so I would wake up drenched in sweat. I was very moody during this period. Because of how much I smoked, I needed to drink as much water and cranberry juice as possible. The days leading up to the screen, I was drinking gallons of water and cranberry juice. I drank so much water and cranberry juice, I ended up getting sick.

I cleaned myself out and got the job, so it was worth it. I was thankful for this opportunity, but in my mind, I knew this wasn't how I was used to making money. I did also have some legitimate hustles to get my money back up, though.

This job was more important than I thought. Everything I wanted before—now I paid cash for—or like every other "drug dealer," I put cars and other things in someone else's name. I couldn't spend like I used to, but I wanted a new vehicle.

Years ago, my father got me into a credit union, and I spoke to the manager. She told me to fill out an application, and I got approved. She asked what kind of car I wanted, so I told her about the Eddie Bauer Expedition. She said she would have the check ready for me so I could go get the car, which surprised me. I knew about having good credit and all that stuff, but I had conditioned myself to think cash was the best way. I mean, that's how everyone (mostly everyone) saw things in the circle I was in. Not hustling weed wasn't so bad.

My first legitimate hustle was flipping houses. My new job had twelve-hour shifts, so I would work four days on, then four days off. It gave me a lot of time for hustling.

I was riding down the street when I saw an OG I used to talk to. He was a legitimate hustler, man, was he a hustler. There were two guys I knew who could get whatever you wanted—and he was one of them. He had many hustles (all legit), and one was flipping houses. He was outside of one of his properties, delegating to the four or five people he had working for him.

I circled the block and then pulled over with the intention of getting some information. Now, I could do what a normal person does and get a realtor, but I knew there was a hustle to it—and I wanted to hustle it!

I hopped out with a smile.

"Ty!" I yelled.

He smiled back and greeted me with the usual, "What's up, baby boy?"

"How are you? What's new?"

"I'm good—and you're looking at it."

He was buying up property everywhere. He also had his own construction company to do the work on the houses that needed it. I told him I wanted to be like him. I expressed my interest in flipping houses since

I wasn't in the game anymore. He didn't hustle but knew I did. He told me I needed to contact his guy in Indianapolis—he would help me with the process. As I put the number in my phone, he told me to remember who I got the number from.

I stayed for a few more minutes, answering questions about the boys and life. I enjoyed talking to Ty. He had always shown me love and looked out for me whenever I needed anything. I shook his hand and thanked him again for the number.

Ron was the guy I was supposed to contact. I called the next day—no answer. So I left a message. It took him about a week to get back with me. He was that busy with all the deals he had going on. He asked me if I had properties already picked out, if I was trying to flip, and so on. I told him what my intentions were, and he said he'd run my credit and see what he could do. He also told me to find a house or two, and depending on my credit, he'd try to make it happen.

Before getting off the phone, he asked if I was trying to take the equity out of the house when I purchased them. Now that's what I wanted to hear. I knew there was a way for me to get some cash when I closed the deal. He said he'd get back to me in a week or so, but in the meantime, I needed to find some properties. If I didn't know where to look, call Ty.

I ended up calling Ty. We set a time and date to meet with a guy who was selling houses, and met at one of the properties he owned. After getting shown around, I was given the price. Ty let me know what it would cost to fix, as well as pointing out what needed fixing. We did the same thing at the next place, and I told Ty I wanted one. Then he surprised me and asked if I wanted both. Of course I did—and with the price, he didn't think it'd be a problem.

About two weeks later, I got a call from Ron. He told me what I needed to do to get the loan approved, and then asked the price of the property. I mentioned that there were two properties when I gave the price. He said he would make it happen.

The plan was to close on both houses at the same time. However, it didn't happen that way, and I had to buy them one at a time—which meant two closing costs. Closing came for the first house, and we did it at Jack's house. Cassie and I got to his house and met his wife at the door. She invited us in and offered us a drink and a place to sit.

Jack was a good old man. He really tried to help me when he sold me his houses. He told me he started buying homes when he was my age, and now that he was at retirement age, he was selling all eighteen of his properties to use as his retirement.

He talked to me for a while, giving me advice about the business. He even told me not to take the equity out of the homes if I didn't have to. He was really trying to help, and I appreciated it a lot. We finished the deal, and I left his house with the keys to my first home—and a check for over twenty thousand dollars.

The second home was already in the works. Less than ten days after I left Jack's house, I had keys to the second house and another check for over twenty thousand dollars.

I was going to rent both of the houses and get another house for me, Cassie, and my boys. On September 6, my third son was born. I knew I had to get a place with Cassie. The best solution was to live in one of the houses and rent the other.

Life was good—but different. I had three boys. I was back with Cassie and promised her I would be the man I once was. Things were okay at home. At least... that's what I thought.

But sometimes, the storm starts brewing just after the sky clears. And I didn't see the clouds coming.

Chapter 16: The Comedy Show

It was time for my next venture. Zay and I weren't talking like we used to, due to him moving to Kentucky and becoming one of Louisville's top DJs. Zay was doing shows with hip-hop artists. After attending some of his events and doing the math, I figured this would be a good way to make some money.

I talked to Zay about throwing a show back home, but he advised against it. He thought I would do better with comedy. I agreed and told him I was going to organize a comedy show in the near future. He said he'd help in any way he could. I didn't want his help, though—not in a negative way. I just wanted to prove I could pull it off myself.

Soon after arriving in Louisville, Zay started Slugga Entertainment. Following his lead, I launched Big Face Entertainment to promote my own events. To get Big Face off the ground, I knew I needed a couple of people to help me. I chose Darin for a couple of reasons: he was my man—I'd known him longer than anyone else I was working with—and he was great with finances, having worked at a bank for years doing accounting. Darin and I would be 50/50 partners in the company.

I also brought in my man Rico. Rico is my son's uncle and a very sharp guy. One day, while telling him about the idea, he sent me several websites within the hour where I could book almost any comedian I wanted. Needless to say, Rico became the COO of Big

Face Ent. This wasn't something we were doing halfway—I even went to a lawyer, on Zay's advice, and had Big Face made into a legitimate business.

First order of business: get a business plan together. I needed to make sure I could afford this before booking comedians, venues, hotels, and everything else. Everyone did their part. Rico found a few options for booking comedians, so I called around and got some quotes. The prices were steep, but I knew once I got them here, I could build relationships and cut out the middleman next time.

We brainstormed every possible expense. Darin came up with a number—the total cost of the show. He and I agreed to split the cost and work out something later for Rico. Darin let me know he might not have the money right away, but he'd come through. I wasn't tripping about the money; I just wanted this event to be a success. The total cost didn't exceed ten thousand dollars, which I had. Plus, I wouldn't have to pay all of it at once.

Once we had pricing sorted, it was time to put the show together. First, I needed a venue. I thought the best place to host it would be the Indiana Theatre, an older building with a classic, vintage vibe. The three of us scheduled an appointment with the building manager to tour the space and get more info—like how many people it could seat. Walking in, it was just like I remembered from my childhood when I went there to see movies.

At the end of the tour, we talked price. It was high, but we agreed. As we were walking out, Rico asked,

"What do you think?" I looked at him and Darin and said, "We throwing a show."

They laughed as we got in the car to discuss our next move: promotion.

We decided we needed flyers, radio spots, and word of mouth. Rico and Darin would handle the radio, while I reached out to Zay about the flyers. He had used professionally made flyers for his shows before. I know I said I didn't want his help, but he was the expert on this part. He offered to get the flyers done for me and save me some money. I sent him the information, and he got the ball rolling.

One afternoon, while I was running basketball practice, I talked to the woman who ran the gym. Her daughter worked at the college radio station. I asked if she thought her daughter would let us promote the show on air—we were willing to pay. I really wanted to tap into the college crowd.

At one of our weekly meetings, I told Rico and Darin I could get us on the ISU campus radio. Rico reached out to the main radio station too, but their price was steep, and after some back and forth, we didn't end up booking it. Still, we did get on the campus radio.

The three of us went to the studio and even called the headliner so he could record a drop to promote the event. He let everyone know he and the other comedians were coming. We also did an interview with the radio host to plug the show. Within a week, I sent Zay the money and received our flyers. In my mind, the major obstacles were handled. Once we locked down the venue, I called LJ and locked in the artists.

With the deposit paid for the comedians, promotion covered, flyers circulating, and our show being promoted on the radio—plus the venue being paid in full—I felt like there wasn't much left. I was wrong.

Darin told me we didn't have any physical tickets, then proceeded to remind me that I hadn't figured out anything as far as security was concerned. I told him I'd handle it. My grandmother's neighbor's son was a police officer. I contacted him and asked if he and another officer would be interested in working our show. He agreed and told me he could get another officer to help out. (I had to pay them, of course.)

We still had to make all the arrangements for the comedians when they came in, too. Most of the time, you'd have to pick them up or rent them a car. We didn't have to do any of that. Since they were coming from Chicago, they decided to drive. We just had to have the rest of their money and a hotel room. Of course, we, being the hosts that we were, offered a couple of other amenities.

Show time.

Everything was set and paid for. I had the money for the comedians when they arrived. I was excited to see what would happen. There weren't many presale tickets, but I was hoping sales would pick up.

I was prepared for the show weeks in advance. I had two different throwbacks to put on—one for the day and one for the show. We bought a fifth of

Belvedere vodka when we purchased the bottles for the comedians. I also had some weed for me and Darin, since Rico didn't smoke.

The day was planned. I'd pick up Darin and Rico in the morning to pass out more flyers. Darin and I were smoking and drinking from the time I picked them up.

We ran some last-minute errands before we had to be at the theater to sell tickets. Still drinking and smoking, we headed to the hotel where the comedians were staying. We went to their rooms to see if they needed anything. There were two male and one female comedian. The two males were playing PlayStation in one room, and the lady was getting settled in the other.

We kicked it for a few minutes, then had to check on the other act. After checking in with Maria, she asked if I had a minute. She asked me some questions about how much we paid down and what the total was. Because we went through a middleman, the split wasn't exactly like the contract stated. She said that's why she liked to book her own events.

She went on to tell me about some of the things that she was doing and said she thought we could make some money with the venue we were renting. She was a hustler, so I could relate. We exchanged numbers and would stay in touch after the show.

We only had a few hours before the show, and ticket sales hadn't picked up much. I went home to clean up and get ready. I picked up Darin, already smoking. We smoked a blunt and headed over to get Rico. We arrived about an hour early to get some music playing and check ticket sales while we were gone.

Not much had changed.

Matter of fact, we didn't exceed three hundred ticket sales.

The show went on anyway and was a success, depending on how you looked at it. The comedians killed it. (Well, two outta the three.) Minus a few things I needed to change, not bad for our first show.

I treated the comedians very well while they were there. I exchanged numbers with all three of them. They knew I lost money on the event, and two of the three told me they would give me a discount and work with me on the next event.

I spoke to both of them and even put money on a show that Maria did—but I never threw another show myself.

Looking back, this was a missed opportunity for me.

I knew exactly what to do to make the next show a success, but I wasn't mature enough yet to run a business like a business.

Instead, I talked Darin into going to Louisville the day after the show to blow the money we had just made... on throwback jerseys.

The lights went out on that stage, but maybe not forever.

Chapter 17: Gambling

After about twenty months at my job, we were called to an off-site meeting place. We were told that if you were hired after a certain date, you were laid off. Well, actually, we were fired. I wasn't sure what to do now. I needed this job. I had two house payments and only one tenant, so I was basically paying both house payments on my own. Soon after I started working, I started gambling again. When I was hustling, I would play PlayStation for money.

I was at Antonio's house one night, and a couple of hustlers were there. They pulled out the dice and asked who wanted some. Three or four dudes got on the floor as one of them rolled the dice on the floor. I got down and pulled out maybe a hundred dollars. We were shooting like five dollars, nothing big. One time, I had the dice and was about to roll when someone said, "Oh, he doesn't want it." I crapped out soon after. I lost all of the money I pulled out before the game was over.

I left Antonio's house that night and went to my parents' house to talk to my dad. I told him I lost one hundred dollars shooting dice. And he laughed and asked if I had some dice. I went and got a set of dice and handed them to him. He showed me a couple of things with the dice. After that, I started having success shooting dice. That night at Antonio's was embarrassing. Not because I lost some money, but because I was playing a game I didn't really know how to play. But I learned to play, and I was going to show it, like the Christmas party at my son's mom's house.

She had a Christmas party every Christmas Eve. This particular year, the dice came out in a back bedroom.

Darin and I were there having a good time, and of course, we wanted the action with the dice. Money didn't matter. Whatever was in my pockets could be lost. It was the total opposite, though. I was hitting everything. Darin had seen this a few times before while we were gambling, so he was betting with me. I remember people laughing and wondering what he knew that they didn't. I gained a lot of respect that night. I don't know what I won that night, but I do know I was the man.

I would often catch a dice game with some of the homies or a casino. Although the rules were different, I even learned how to make a couple of dollars at the casino. I didn't do as well as I did on the streets, but I would often come home a winner. That doesn't mean I never lost, though.

When I was hustling, it was okay because I wasn't hurt by the money I spent gambling, but it was different once I started working again. I really didn't have the extra money to waste on a gambling habit. I would go two or three times a month. I even got my Pops to go with me quite a few times. We would go so much that the table workers knew us. Cassie and I went to the casino on many occasions, both when I was hustling and when I was working. Once working, however, I wouldn't take as much money to gamble with. I even gave her money to put away so I wouldn't gamble it all. There were times I lost what I had and "needed" some more money. She would give it to me. The outcome determined the ride home. If I lost, we fought. If I won, she would still be mad I didn't stop when I said I would, but it wasn't a fight.

After losing my job at PolyOne, I started working at Sony in production as a machine operator. This was a good job for the area. I was still working nights, four days on and four days off. It still gave me the time to do what I wanted outside of work.

Chapter 18: Ball is Back

Dre was four, so I decided to sign him up at the Boys Club and see how it went. I always knew I wanted to coach my kids. There were a few reasons I wanted to coach them. The most important was to build the same relationship with them that I had with my father. We have great memories from the court. It was just me and him—real father-and-son time. I also wanted to make sure if they were good enough, they would get their chance. Them playing point guard was something else I wanted. Being a good two guard was cool until you went to the top sixty workout and only got the ball twice, but the point guards got all the shots, and the ones they didn't take, they passed to the big man.

I worked on his ball handling and his shot almost every day on his little goal we had at the house. He scored and was advanced for a four-year-old. I coached him from K-2 at the Boys Club before I started coaching AAU Basketball. Jayden was playing at the Boys Club too, and he loved it, so I decided to put him on the AAU team as well. I explained to him how everyone was older and he wouldn't play very much. He didn't care. He just wanted to be on the team.

Although they were three years apart, my son Jayden started school a year early, so they were only two grades apart. I caught a lot of slack for putting him on a team that much older than him, though. His mom and family weren't happy. She wanted him to play with kids his age. She wasn't happy with the way he was shooting the ball either. Because he was smaller than everyone else, he would shoot the ball behind his head. I tried to explain to her that I would change his shot and he would be just fine.

He continued to play with his brother for the next few years. We didn't just play basketball, though. I had them running hills and jumping boxes and rope. All of this was done at six in the morning. They could shoot after running. I wanted them to be in good shape as well as being able to play the game. They did it all. They didn't have any problems doing what I asked them to do, but they didn't like it either. They didn't enjoy getting up at six o'clock every morning in the summer. Since I was working from six p.m. to six a.m., I would pick them up after work. Of course, I caught slack for doing all of this.

When Dre was in the third grade, I started an AAU team with a guy I met at the Boys Club while the basketball season was going on. For both of us, this was our first time coaching AAU. He told me he wanted to take care of the administrative things and I could be the head coach. I didn't mind because I didn't care who set up tournaments or things like that. All I wanted to do was coach.

I had both of my kids on this team. However, I knew that my youngest son wasn't going to get a lot of time on the court. I just wanted him to be in the gym as much as possible. He loved being a part of the team with the older boys, no matter how much he played. This team had most of the talent in that age group too. I got killed as a coach in my very first game by over twenty points, though. I learned so much from that first game. Basketball had to be played 365 days a year. There were kids playing every day and teams that had been together since first or second grade. So I figured if WE kept these kids together, we could compete and beat some of these teams that killed us in my first tournament.

After a very shaky beginning, things looked like they were going to come together. The next season at the Boys Club, we had to draft the kids that we wanted on our team. The other coach and I made an agreement to not draft the kids that we had on each other's teams the year prior. I was in for a surprise on draft night. The guy I was coaching with decided to take a couple of the players I had coached the year before. There were two other kids that I planned on getting, and some other coaches took them. This should have taught me something. I should have known that some people were more worried about winning than anything. I should have understood that it is what it is. It was just youth basketball, and I should have treated it as such. This was a lesson I would learn a year to a year and a half later.

I took the players I had and we made the most of it. Since the team wasn't very good, it allowed my oldest son a chance to take a leadership role. It was also a chance for my youngest son to get some experience playing with older kids. We probably lost more games than we should have.

Right before the season was over, I had a parent ask me about AAU practice and why I wasn't there. Truthfully, I wasn't even aware of the practice. I felt disrespected. I was the head coach and had two kids on the team—and they weren't invited to practice with the team they were on. Honestly, that made me more upset than the fact that I wasn't asked to attend. So, I decided to start my own organization. I would pick the kids I wanted and play in the tournaments.

I wasn't the only person with a team. There were at least three or four different teams in that age group, so there was a battle to get the best kids. After putting everything together (with the help of a parent of a kid on the team), this team that started with just three or four kids turned into a very aggressive and talented group of fourth graders.

The hunger these kids showed was inspiring to me. I pushed this team harder than any team I've coached to date.

The fourth-grade team came along well. Both the kids and all the families got along great. We also got a lot of support from the community. I was getting money from businesses to sponsor the team. Many of the parents went out of their way to help—raising funds, getting uniforms sponsored, and doing whatever they could. We played in many tournaments that year and had a lot of success, thanks in part to them.

My big man wasn't very experienced. In fact, it was his first year playing. He was our only big man, but I had some guards who were very aggressive. I would yell, "Who wants to play?" when they were on defense, and they'd slap the floor and drop into a stance. We pressured the ball similar to what my favorite college team, Louisville, would do.

Most teams had more solid big men, which meant we struggled at times with rebounding and stopping opposing centers. Still, we were winning. I thought everyone was happy.

After doing well in local and surrounding area tournaments, we made it to the state tournament. Things went great—we placed sixth.

While there, a few things happened that made me feel like this was as good as youth basketball could get. The parents made sure the kids had everything they needed. After games, we'd go out to eat as a team, and a parent would often pick up the entire tab. After one loss, the kids were back at the hotel pool like nothing had happened. I went down to check on them and was surprised to see them laughing and having a great time. They weren't even worried about the loss. Honestly, I took it worse than they did.

To top it off, our big man had really come into his own by the time we left the Statetournament. That growth was great to see.

As I was leaving the gym on the last dayof the tournament , a parent whose son played for another team approached me. They liked what I had done with my group and asked if there was room for their son. I told them yes—and that I'd be in touch when we started back up.

The next year looked real promising to me. We had a strong team, and the addition of the new kids was going to make us one of the best teams in the state. We had some shooters (including my son), a couple of guys who could get to the basket, and our point guard was also a football player. He was a very aggressive kid. He had no fear going to the basket, he could handle the ball, and he gave me 110% every game. I gave this kid a lot of freedom. I let him do pretty much what he wanted to do. He would also push the ball like I asked him to.

My oldest son was a shooter, but he didn't handle the ball as well, and he wasn't as aggressive. So this kid had more freedom than my son. I bring this up because there had been talk over the years that "Bernie just coaches for his kids." This was my first team, and my son wasn't the focal point. When I started coaching, I wanted to make sure there were certain things my kids got as basketball players. However, I am fair. I worked my kids very hard, and with that, they should be able to hold their own. As a coach, I wasn't going to give my son the ball just because he's my son.

This team was very successful and one of the most competitive teams I'd ever coached to date. My assistant coach told me he thought we should start more teams in different age groups, so that's what we planned to do. We had enough kids to start three different teams. My assistant coach actually gave me the idea to take on a high school team. I was undecided at first, but I thought it would be a challenge to coach older kids, so I agreed to it.

Everything started out well, and I was getting support from many people. I put my all into this AAU organization. I was volunteering my time, money, and most importantly—my heart.

My love for the sport finally came back. I was enjoying my time around these kids, teaching them the game of basketball. I also realized there was another way to give back.

I began mentoring some of the kids I was coaching.

And in those moments—on hardwood floors, surrounded by passion, sweat, and promise—I found something deeper than wins. I found purpose.

Chapter 19: Tiny

I started late with the high school team and couldn't put them in a tournament the first year. I did have them practice and worked on their game before the season started. I still remember that first practice. I set it up myself. I received all the numbers from one kid on the team whose father was a good friend of mine.

Once I received the names and numbers of the possible players, I realized I knew the mother or father of most of these kids. I called to let all the players know when and where to be and to bring a parent so I could hold a parent meeting. I also told them we would have a quick practice that same night.

I spoke to the parents first, and everything went smoothly. I was raised to respect my elders, and I demanded respect from every player I coached. After the meeting, some parents stayed to ask questions. When I got to the last parent, it wasn't actually a parent but a grandparent. The man was very nice and just wanted to know about something I had covered in the meeting. His grandson (my new player) was telling him to leave and not to worry about it. I thought the kid was a spoiled young man and wouldn't talk that way around me. I didn't think we would work well together.

I hadn't seen any of these kids play—I had just gotten back into watching basketball when I started the AAU organization—but I had heard about most of them. I had them do some basic drills before I had them scrimmage. I have to admit, I couldn't wait to see them in action.

Once they started, I was most impressed by the young man I had heard the least about. This young man had the most heart of any soon-to-be freshman that I had seen. He was also a shooter like I was. The difference between his game and mine was how well he could handle the ball, but he wasn't playing above the rim like I did. This was also the young man who was getting smart with his grandfather before practice. I saw a lot of myself in this young man, and I really wanted to help him so he wouldn't make the same mistakes I made.

I began to develop a mentor relationship with this young man. I would talk to him often, giving him advice. I wanted to make sure that he was putting up enough shots, and I also wanted him to do some of the things that I did so he could start dunking and playing above the rim. So the summer before his high school season, I asked his mother if I could mentor him while working on his game. She was very accepting of me trying to help her son. We were on the same page as we both wanted what was best for the young man.

I was already taking my sons to the park to shoot every morning, so I would go get him and have him shoot as well. I decided to have him run hills and jump boxes like I did when my vertical really improved. My oldest kids were also running hills and jumping the boxes too. After doing this, I would then take them to the park where they would shoot hundreds of shots before we would go back to my house, where I would cook them some bacon, eggs, and toast. Then I would take him back home.

I spent a lot of time with this young man. I went to his summer games, and I would tell him how I thought he played.

My cousin had a celebrity birthday party with Jadakiss, the multi-platinum rapper. I had already made plans to go, but I thought it would be a good experience for him to meet a rapper he listened to. We went to the party and even got a chance to meet and walk around the mall with Jadakiss.

I would also take him to church with me. At one point, I was taking three or four different kids to church with me. I did little things for him too, like getting him some t-shirts when I went out of town. I would offer to buy him a pair of shoes if he had so many points, and things like that.

At one point, he had to have surgery on his shoulder and I had to work the night before. I went up there right after work and stayed until he came out. I went back to see him when he came out of surgery, and he was still half out of it. I joked with him and went home to get some sleep for work the next day.

We would continue to work out that summer and build a big brother/little brother relationship. I felt like I was really making a difference. Right or wrong, I felt that by helping as many of these young men as possible, I was giving back for everything I'd done in my younger days. Sure, the basketball was good and I was trying to give back with the AAU, but I realized I could do more by mentoring as many young men as I could. If I could keep some of them from selling and/or using drugs, or abusing alcohol, I felt I was giving back.

It wasn't just the one young man (Tiny) that I was mentoring or working out. I think he felt more comfortable if he had a friend or two there with him. So he would often bring a friend to the workouts, and they would also go back to the house to eat on multiple occasions.

I really thought this kid had what it took to play Division 1 basketball. However, on July 29, 2009, his life would change forever. His girlfriend gave birth to a little boy that day, and he would now have to try to support a son and play ball at the same time. Tiny was seventeen years old at the time—and now a father.

Our relationship was very strong at this time. However, we weren't working out like we used to because he now had a responsibility. He was a father. When he couldn't work out, it was because he had to work or watch his son. I knew how much he needed to be working out, but I really respected the way he wanted to be the best father he could be. However, there were times I felt he could have worked out and he used his son as an excuse.

Later, I was offered the opportunity to be an assistant coach for the high school he was attending. I was currently coaching at the junior high school my son was playing at. I received a call from Tiny, asking me if I wanted to be an assistant at the high school and, if I was interested, to call the coach.

The head coach was an assistant when I was playing at the same high school. I called him and he told me he would like for me to be a part of the program and continue to help the young men I had been helping. He also told me it would be good to have me around because of my relationship with Tiny and some of the other players.

I do believe me being on the bench helped during Tiny's last two years of high school, even if he wasn't consistent. He would put up thirty one night and fifteen the next. I had the same issues with being consistent, so it was frustrating because I knew it was a lack of work in the off-season. All I could do was encourage him. I understood when he couldn't make it because he was watching his son, but a part of me just wanted him to be there.

Overall, he had a good high school career, though. He scored over nine hundred points, played as a freshman, and was one of the area's best when he graduated. He wasn't getting the offers that I thought he would get from colleges, but he did get a chance to play at ICC.

And for me, watching him walk across that stage, diploma in hand and his son in the crowd, felt like a different kind of victory. Not every success story ends in a trophy or scholarship offer. Sometimes, it ends in knowing a young man made it—because someone believed he could.

Chapter 20: Joe Jackson

When my second son was young, maybe like eight or nine years old, his mother started calling me Joe Jackson, insinuating that I was too hard on Jay like Joe was on Michael. I took my kids to shoot like my father did with me, but I took it a step further. I would have them doing boxes like I did in high school. I would also have them running hills, then we would shoot and do some ball-handling drills. Of course, this was all in the summer when they didn't have school. I would get off of work at six a.m. and get the boys up then we would go hit the hills.

Jay didn't live with me, and his mother thought he was too young to be running hills. So, many times when I went to pick him up, we would go back and forth, disagreeing about how hard I was pushing him at that age. It didn't stop me. I continued to make him run the hills and work out in the mornings.

I was using the community center to have team practices, so they would still have to go to the gym later with me and either practice or work out again. They were real gym rats. And I pushed them to the limit. I wanted them prepared for whatever. I wanted them to outwork everyone on the court. I also wanted them to be mentally prepared.

I was harder on them than any of the other kids I coached. I wanted to be the hardest coach they ever played for. If they could handle everything I threw at them, they'd be able to handle anything any other coach threw! This caused fights between me and Jay's mother. The harder I pushed, the more we would fight. This was where I got the name Joe Jackson. I was "too hard," and this and that.

It got to the point where she would call me Joe Jackson so much that other people (especially people in her family) would call me Joe Jackson. The name stuck, and some people still say, "Hey, Joe," when they see me at games.

And maybe they're not wrong. Maybe I was too hard sometimes. But when I look back, I don't just see drills or sweat or arguments—I see effort. I see love, buried in tough lessons. I see a father doing everything he could to raise boys into men who could stand tall in any gym, any game, any moment. And if that makes me Joe Jackson, so be it. But mine was never about fame. It was about preparing them for a world that wouldn't go easy—and making sure they could take the shot when it mattered most.

Chapter 21. Lessons Beyond the Court

My oldest son was in the sixth grade, playing at his junior high school. He was also starting for his team. He had twenty points in his first junior high school game. He was 4-5 from the three-point line. My cousin was his coach. He asked me to help out with the team since I had coached some of them in AAU. I agreed to be the assistant on the sixth-grade team. The kids had a decent year, but couldn't win the county championship. Dre played well. He shot the ball very well. Actually, he broke the record for the most three-pointers in a season.

Jayden was now in the fourth grade. I had a little work to do with him. Before that summer, Jayden was shooting the ball over his head. Because of all the And 1 videos he watched and his desire to mimic those moves, he had nice ball-handling skills. It was crazy how he was able to hit those shots with the way he was shooting. However, it was time to change his shot and get the ball in front of him, not over his head. I planned on playing him in his own age group instead of with the older kids, so I knew he would be able to get his shot off easier, plus he couldn't shoot like that forever. I changed his shot and he had a solid year at the boys' club.

I started with Carver playing the game young. I had him in the gym as much as the other boys or more. He went to all of his brothers' games. He was in the gym more than the other two. He was two-balling in kindergarten. He was the most aggressive of the three, and to be honest, I thought he could be the best of them. He wasn't like the other boys when

I got on him, though. He didn't take it like the other boys. The more I pushed him, the more he would pull away from the game.

I figured I would play him up a grade or two like I did with Jayden. It worked for Jayden, and when Carver was in the second grade, I played him up two grades. He played hard and held his own. I believe that he, being the youngest and always fighting or being picked on by his older brothers, became so aggressive. Luckily, I'd always been able to reel my kids in if they were getting too aggressive or ready to fight or just playing out of character.

Occasionally, I wouldn't be able to make a game because of my work schedule, and my assistant coach would fill in. I missed one game the first year when Carver played. My assistant coach also happened to be my barber. I called after the game from work, and he said everything went well, but Carver was out of character. I asked if I could get a haircut the next day, and he said yes, and he would tell me about what happened. The next day, I went to his house to find out what he meant by my boy being out of character. I got in the chair and we went right into it.

He started laughing before telling me how my son looked like he was playing football and not basketball. Carver jumped on kids' backs for rebounds they had already secured, fouled players hard, or he was just being overaggressive. I'd seen him like that, but not to the extreme he was talking about. Then again, I could reel him in before he got to that point. But I believe this was the point where he realized he really didn't want to play basketball. We finished the season, but I noticed a difference in Carver. He was still his aggressive self. He just wasn't into the game. He didn't watch it like the other boys. He didn't want to talk about it like the other boys. And when I tried to talk to him about basketball. he didn't seem interested. I was disappointed but thought it would pass and he would eventually start to take an interest like the other boys.

Toward the end of the summer, he started to miss workouts. Carver was spending more time at my in-laws instead of my parents with the other boys. When all three of them were together, they fought and argued like most boys their age. And I'm sure the older two would pick on Carver on occasion. By spending more time with my father-in-law, though, he started to pick up other hobbies, things that were different than his brothers. He liked the outdoors, using his hands, and didn't mind getting dirty. Carver just liked to dance to the beat of his own drum.

Right before my sixth season as a coach was over, I started to prepare for the AAU season for my oldest son and the team that had so much success the previous year. I called my assistant coach and the man helping me with the organization to have a sit-down so we could discuss the upcoming season. This meeting was just like every other pre-season meeting. He sounded excited to get things going.

Once the boys' club season was over, I called some of the kids to see if they would be available for practice. As I spoke to many of my players' parents, they told me they didn't know who they would be playing for. It was between me and another organization. After hearing this from a few of the parents, I thought I'd better call my assistant to see what he heard. I knew his son wasn't going anywhere. He was my assistant, not just in coaching, but with the whole organization. His son was the leader of the team, and I made sure to give his son a lot of freedom.

When I called him, he never said anything about his mind being made up to have his son play on this other team. I still had a few more kids to call. I called another parent whose son was a starter. He told me the truth. He told me that the assistant coach's son wasn't playing with me. He told me that many of the kids have already made arrangements to play on this other team. After calling all the parents, I lost every kid on this team besides my own. I must admit it bothered me. I thought I did something wrong. I questioned myself and the way I was coaching. I blamed myself for my son not getting a chance to play AAU that year. After really thinking the whole thing through, I had to look at it two ways. If a parent didn't think I was doing the best with their kids, then they *should* have taken their kids to someone else. I also had to remember it was youth basketball and to treat it as such.

There were a few teams in that age group, so I had a hard time getting players. This was frustrating mainly because my son wasn't getting a chance to play. I knew he needed to play, but I couldn't get a team together for him, so I just kept him in the gym. We worked on his game during the summer when the other kids were playing AAU. Years later, I spoke to the man running the team that had most of my players. He said that he wanted my team, but my assistant coach told him I didn't want my son to play. He said since we lived around the corner from each other, he had already spoken to me about my son playing on that team. On the other hand, I had never heard anything from this man. I wasn't surprised to find this out, though. If someone would talk to all the parents on my team to get them to switch teams without my knowledge, why would I be shocked he didn't want my son on this team? I was learning to put more time into my own children since other parents didn't want me to coach their children.

The following summer was different for me because neither of my older sons had a team to play on. I also had a high school team now. I ended up coaching at a youth center, and my boys played on my team. I had a guy talk to me about putting four kids I had and four he had and make a team, but that never panned out. Our schedules wouldn't allow us to meet like we needed to and we just stopped communicating. I would continue to work with my boys individually too. We still hit the gym three or four days a week, plus we would play at different parks.

Both of the boys' games really started to develop now. Dre was still working hard for me. Jayden, on the other hand, was not only working hard for me, but he had turned into a real gym rat. His confidence level was at one hundred. One thing I learned from coaching my kids was the advantages of playing them up a grade or two. I actually played Jayden three years up (he started school early). That wasn't a popular decision with most parents, but I'm glad I stuck with it. Now that he had grown some more and he was shooting the ball well (and correctly), when he played at the youth center with the older guys, he was confident he was able to play with them. It didn't hurt that he had been playing with and against his older brother all his life. And at this point, they were starting to battle. He still couldn't beat Dre consistently, but he'd given him all he had. Dre, on the other hand, wouldn't let little brother win (for the most part). Jayden would win every now and then, and Dre would be very upset. Jayden wouldn't win that often, but he was also just as mad that he didn't win. I tried to explain to him (although he knew) that Dre was older and was supposed to win. He didn't want to hear it. He had a real passion for the game, plus he was a sore loser. All of my boys were sore losers. They hated to lose. I was the same way.

I received a call from my man Marcus asking what I was doing. He told me he had a friend of his who was a coach from up north who had worked some Nike camps with some big names. He was in town for a wedding, and when Marcus told him about the boys, he wanted to see what they could do. He sent Zack my number, and he hit me up right away. It was a Sunday. I didn't have any gym time on Sunday and didn't know where I could take them. I decided to call a guy who worked at the youth center I used to go to, and told him the situation and he let us in.

Zack worked the boys hard, and they worked hard for him. At this point, not too many people were working with my boys. So, it was good to see them take instructions from someone else. He had them doing different drills than I had them doing, so they struggled until they had a chance to do it a couple of times. I was happy with the way the workout went. He had them doing a lot of different shooting drills. They shot the ball well, very well, during the workout. I got the feedback from Zack and it was what I had thought about them. Dre was a hell of a shooter, but needed to work on his ball-handling. It was solid but not on A-string. Jayden was also a hell of a shooter, and his ball-handling was closer to being on A-string at this time. Zack saw something in both boys. He talked about how well they shot the ball, but he said he thought Jayden could be special. He told me he would keep me in mind when there were camps or workouts that might benefit the boys.

As Jay entered fifth grade and Dre entered seventh, they started to come into their own. Dre came off a good year. He broke the junior high school record for three-pointers made in a season. Jayden's game was getting stronger. Being younger, I saw some things he needed to work on, but his game was starting to come together nicely. The junior high school season was a joke, though. They didn't play over ten games. The schools didn't busy the kids to the games. There was only a week of tryouts and a week or two of practice before the season started. Nevertheless, I agreed to help out once again with the now seventh-graders. We were about a week into practice and one week before our first game when I got a call from Tiny. He asked if I would like to sit on the bench. I laughed.

He said, "No, for real. Coach told me to call you to see if you're interested and if you are, to give him a call." I said okay, and he asked if I was going to help out. I said yes again. I called the coach and told him I spoke to Tiny and asked if he really had a position open. He did, and I could start immediately.

I was excited to start working with the high school young men. Contrary to popular belief, I wanted to stop coaching my oldest son during school ball and just coach him in AAU. I knew I couldn't coach all my boys when they got to that point, so I decided that's when I'd let them go and let someone else coach them. I thought it would be a good opportunity since I had coached many of these boys. I really enjoyed being on the bench for the high school games. I also spent some time outside of practice talking to the coach. Most of the time, he would call me and ask me what I thought about either a team, a player, or if I thought something might work. If I didn't give him the answer he wanted, I would have to convince him I was right; if not, he would go with his instincts. I learned a lot from the coach and could have learned so much more had we not had a short run and he had not gotten sick.

One thing I liked about this coach was that he tried to be fair. Some players had longer leashes; they were better ball players. Before he got sick, he told me, "I know you work with your boys. Make sure they are ready when they get here." I understood what he was saying. Although I was on the staff, my kids wouldn't play unless they were ready. I was one step ahead of the coach, I thought. Not only would they be ready, they'd be three times better than everyone else. Where I come from, being an African-American male in high school, it was thought you had to be three times better than everyone else to make sure you could play. I won't get into whether or not that's true (right now).

The high school team would have morning practices three or four days a week. Since I got off work at six a.m., I would volunteer to run those practices for the coach. It was more opportune for my boys to get some shots in. I would get off, pick them up, and head to the gym where I would turn the lights on, lower the goals, and get the team going on what the coach wanted them to work on. My boys knew the routine. Some ball handling, then shots. Sometimes, if we didn't have enough time, it was just shots! After talking to the coach for a few minutes when he showed up, I would rush off to get the boys to school.

The high school season didn't go as well as we would have liked. To be honest, it wasn't the best team, and the players we had really didn't put the necessary time in over the summer. I hate to admit it, but that also included Tiny. Tiny had an okay season but was very short of his potential. The season was short, too. We lost in the sectionals.

The next year was different in many ways. Dre was working out with me, but not on an AAU team. I struggled to put something together for him again that year. He had a team or two ask him to play and he decided not to. He and I decided we would spend more time in the gym working on his game and preparing him for high school. Of course, I wanted him to play. But when I couldn't put anything together, I didn't want him to get down. Instead, I wanted him to get better. He worked hard that summer, but not hard enough. Dre was very athletic for his build and could shoot the ball very well. However, Dre needed to work on some things on his own. I would take them to the gym or a park and work on their games, but now it was time to show how bad they wanted it.

Dre decided to spend his spare time doing other things. He was a teenager now and wanted to hang out and do things that teenagers did. I allowed him to. I didn't force him to go play basketball when he wanted to hang out. As long as he was working out with me and staying out of trouble, I was fine with it.

Okay, I wasn't. I was pissed. Why was this kid not in the gym?! I asked him repeatedly, and no matter the excuse, I could see the "love" for the game vanishing away. Don't get me wrong, he really, really liked it. But he just didn't love it enough. Or he loved it but *wasn't in* love with it.

Either way, it wasn't enough for me. But I always wanted my boys to make their own decisions. I NEVER wanted to live through my boys, so when Dre didn't do the extras, I didn't make him. I tried to advise him that he was approaching high school and he needed to be three times better than everyone else, especially if I was coaching. He would always tell me he was going to, but never did on his own. Of course, I made him work out with me. If you're going to play—and he said he wanted to—then you had to work on your game.

Jayden, on the other hand, was very different at this point. By now (in fifth grade), he had the ball on a string. He could shoot it, too. But his biggest attribute was his confidence. A pastor friend of mine was running a camp at the youth center and asked me to bring the boys down. I agreed. At this point, I liked to let them play and see how they did later. Especially if it wasn't a "real" game, I would drop in on some practices or open gyms, but I wanted them to be free and try things they may not have if I was there.

I dropped them off and went back home. A couple of hours later, I showed up a little early to talk to my man about how they did. I waited around while the boys shot around as the gym started to empty. I told the boys to come on and I motioned for my man to call me after he got finished. And we walked out. My boys couldn't wait to tell me how they did when I wasn't around. We didn't even get to the car, and they were already telling us how the camp went. When they were kids, they would always cut each other off, never letting the other finish a sentence. But now, they'd let the other talk, starting when the other took a break.

I decided to go to my parents' house after I picked the boys up. As we pulled up to my parents' house, my phone rang, cutting one of the boys off from their story. It was my man calling from the camp. He had a funny story to tell me. Jayden was sitting on the stage (right next to the court), hopped down in his socks before he put his shoes on while the ball was at the other end, ran on the court, and yelled "None of y'all can hold me!" He continued by saying how well he played and how the older kids had issues guarding him. I laughed, but not because he was trash-talking. I laughed because I knew his confidence was growing, and he wasn't the same little guy they had played with before. He knew how to use what he had learned being younger and smaller than everyone else. But it wasn't just his age that made him play a different way. He was a little chubby and not as fast as a lot of the other kids, so he would do little things like shot fakes, ball fakes, and hesitate to get an advantage. His game was coming together. But he had to get in better shape.

I got a call from Zack out of the blue asking if we were interested in coming up for a camp the following weekend. He said to bring both boys, and when we got there, to tell them that he sent us and everything would be taken care of. Zack did a lot of things in the Chicago area. Sometimes the events would be in Indiana, but close to Chicago. I didn't really want to go that far for a camp, but I thought it would be good for them to play against some Chicago-area players. I told him we would be there.

We had almost a three-hour drive there, and it was a two or three-hour camp. My pops went with us. He didn't miss much when it came to the boys. After a long drive, we arrived about nine or ten in the morning. I can't remember exactly what time it started, but we were early, really early. There were some guys there setting things up, but no players. We had a ball in the car, so the boys shot around for a while. I had to tell them to sit for a while, or they would have shot until camp started. They rested for a while, then went back out to get warmed up before the camp began.

They were itching to get back out there. I let them go back out about twenty minutes before the camp began. After about five minutes, a young man came and got the boys registered. They were mad that they couldn't continue to shoot. They were shooting good, so I told them to save some of those shots for the camp. After they registered, we sat for a few minutes before they gathered everyone around and gave the "before the camp" spiel. After that, they did some warmup stuff, a little ball handling, and then they split into teams.

Dre was on the court with the first team. As they were doing the lay-up line right before the game, I was approached by a gentleman who was a head coach for a local school. He introduced himself and asked if I was the father of the boys from Terre Haute. He continued to tell me how Zack spoke highly of them, especially their shooting.

The players and refs were on the court and the game was about to begin. The team Dre was on got the tip, marking the first possession of the game. They moved the ball one pass to the wing to Dre for three. Next possession, he got the ball in transition and pulled up about three feet from the three-point line. The very next possession, the ball swung to the left side of the court. Someone screened for Dre on the opposite side of the court. He came off the screen, but his defender was right up on him, so he had to go out by the volleyball line. When he caught the ball, he didn't hesitate and hit his third three-pointer in three possessions, each one further out.

Coach Travis tapped me on the shoulder and said he would be right back. He had an AAU coach that he wanted to see Dre play. He returned without the coach, saying he hadn't made it to the gym yet. Dre played well in the second half. He did other things besides scoring the ball. Plus, he wasn't getting the ball like he did in the first half. The coach told me after the game that he would contact the coach and tell him about Dre.

On a different court, Jayden was about to play his first game of the day. Jayden was on it from the beginning. He had the ball in his hands from the start of the game. He was facilitating and not really looking to score, until the guy he was guarding hit a three. Jayden, in return, came down and hit one right back. The other young man hit another three right after Jayden. He came down and followed his with a deep three, with a hand in his face. They went back and forth a few times during the game.

Both boys had a good showing at the camp. After the camp, Coach Travers and I exchanged numbers. He would stay in touch with the team for Dre.

That year was my last year on the high school varsity bench. We lost most of the scoring from the previous year.

The team wasn't very good, and we struggled because of that. The coach also let everyone know he was sick and that this would be his last year. While my time there was brief, I learned a lot. Of course, that included the basketball aspect, but there's more to high school basketball than just basketball. (Well, at least where I'm from.) I won't go into detail (now), but the coach and I spent some time discussing these things. He shared some things with me that gave proof to what we'd been saying for years.

Dre's eighth-grade year was much like the other two. He had a solid season, but he wasn't dominating like I thought he could. His shoot was there; he just didn't handle the ball like he could have, and he didn't drive to the basket enough as well. He did do other things, though. He was a good defender, he passed well when given the opportunity, and he would do a lot of little things that may not show up in the box scores. Just knowing that he needed to be more consistent, I made a plan to work him out harder this year than any other year to prepare him for high school.

I can remember Jayden's first junior high game as well. He played very well: shot the ball well, handled the ball well, and made some very good passes. He looked good! He was slow, though, one of the slowest on the court. I knew that he was chubby and I knew that he had a hard time keeping up as a youngster, but he had grown since then, and I thought he would be in better shape than he was before. I had my work cut out for me over the summer. Jayden would work his butt off during the basketball part of working out, he wasn't big on the non-basketball stuff.

I got the boys back out on the hills. I put together a workout designed to have Dre jumping out of the gym and have Jayden in shape, and add a little quickness to his games.

But it wasn't just the workouts or the hills. Jayden liked to eat! Until now, I never said anything about how much he ate, but I started to monitor his calorie intake. I stopped letting him eat for no reason or have seconds or thirds when his first serving was a healthy portion. I never kept him from eating, but I would sometimes remind him how much work it was going to take to work off all the extras he was eating. That worked! This kid started watching what he was eating himself. He wouldn't ask for seconds as much as he used to and hardly ever asked for thirds.

With Dre going into high school and the coach retiring, I wasn't sure if I would be asked to come back. To be honest, I didn't know if I wanted to coach my boys in high school. I wanted them to get everything they deserved without having to hear anything about their dad being the coach. Plus, they were almost where they needed to be on the court. Nevertheless, once the new coach was announced, I didn't receive a call one way or the other. I waited a few weeks, and still got no call. So, as open gyms started with the new coach, I decided to go speak to him about my position as assistant coach. Without looking me in my eyes, he said he wanted me as the assistant coach, but others didn't. I was mad and my pride got hurt. I thought I was a good coach. I thought I did my part. And I had boys coming up in this same system, so why wouldn't they want me to coach? Well, I spoke to others, trying to figure out who didn't want me to coach and why. All the way up to the superintendent of the school corporation. Once I was led to him, I thought I would be good. He knew me. I'd worked with his nephews. Not just coaching them, but his nephews attended many of my free workouts in the summer. The older one even played on my midnight basketball team. I thought he would see what I was doing for the kids, and would want me to be part of the program. I was terribly wrong.

I set up a meeting with him early one morning. When I walked in, he had a surprised look on his face. Although I thought I had told his secretary the reason for this meeting, I began by explaining to him that I was told he didn't want me on the bench. He laughed and said he didn't have anything to do with him. He continued to tell me the coach didn't want me on the bench and he picked his assistants and that was that. After about two minutes of him talking, I knew what was going on. They were going to blame each other and I was to guess who was telling the truth. It didn't really matter, though. I took the job to help Tiny in the first place. I spent a lot of time in the gym away from home. With morning practice, and games you had to love what you did because it wasn't worth the money. I did enjoy my time as an assistant coach, however, I believe everything happens for a reason.

Once the coach retired and they hired the new coach, things were different. The old coach knew the game. He also cared about the kids and took pride in getting them into school. This new guy? Not so much. Not only that, he didn't know the game, nor could he relate to the kids. He was a smart guy, just not basketball smart.

Dre had a tolerable year. It was really up and down. He had some games that were stat stuffers, playing really well, and there were nights where he looked like an average high school basketball player. He wasn't as consistent as he should have been. There were mental things going on as well. There were three or four freshmen who were moved up to junior varsity from day one. (Actually, I think it was the second day of practice, and the coach sent for them so they could play JV.) Dre came home, and he told me how everyone got moved up, and he didn't. I reminded him about what I had been saying up to this point. He needed to be three times better than everyone else. Was he? No. Should he have been moved up with or before the other boys? Yes.

I knew the freshman coach. His kids attended my wife's daycare. Even though he was a good guy, I just don't think he had total control of his team. We talked a couple of times throughout the season. Midway through the season, they moved up two or three more kids. I had to ask, why not Dre? Well, he didn't know. The coach didn't give an explanation when he told him to send the kids up. There's no doubt that Dre should have been moved up, and I felt he wasn't getting what he had worked for. At the same time, Dre didn't put the extra time in like he wanted it. He would practice and he would work out with me, but he was not going out of his comfort zone and working on his game like he should have.

Jayden was in the seventh grade now. He was a totally different kid. He was a gym rat and a good ball player. He liked to go to the community center after school. And he would play wherever there was a basketball game. His seventh-grade year was better than his sixth, because his body had changed. His knowledge of the game was through the roof, too. Like I said, a totally different kid.

Chapter 22. Lost Control

My attitude had changed a lot over the years. I got married in May of 2007 and had my fourth son in November. I was still working in the same factory and was still coaching basketball for multiple teams. I hadn't been gambling or going out. Things at home should have been good, right? Well, I thought so too. I did not realize I was so focused on my boys that I didn't give my wife the time or attention she deserved. There were many times we had plans to go out to eat or see a movie, and I spent that time in the gym or meeting with someone concerning basketball. She would often go with me and she didn't complain, but I could see that at times it bothered her.

I wouldn't say my wife and I had a rocky relationship; I would just say that we had some issues to work through. We were arguing more and just couldn't seem to get on the same page. If you asked my wife, she may have said something different. She may have said I wasn't the person I once was. Or that although I may had grown as a father and as a man, I hadn't grown as a husband. And those things were true. I hadn't been the most loving husband I could have been. For example, my wife's brother passed, and the viewing was scheduled for Friday, and the funeral was Saturday. Well, that Saturday was the Kentucky Derby. I already had plans for the Derby before I knew there would be a funeral. I asked my wife if she wanted me to stay and go to the funeral with her, and she said it didn't matter to her if I stayed or went since I already had plans. Because I was selfishly thinking of myself, I went to the Derby. I mean, she said it was up to me and she wouldn't be mad, right? I wasn't fair when it came to the holidays, either. We would usually go to my parents' house first. Then we would go to her parents' house. The problem was, sometimes I didn't make it to her parents' house.

I also had an issue with dates. You know, like anniversaries, Mother's Day, and birthdays. For the first couple of years, I thought our anniversary was a day later than it actually was. It's not hard to imagine how my wife must have felt when she would have something for me waiting when I got off work, and I had nothing for her. I tried to make it up by spending more on her or getting her something she really wanted. I thought that would make up for being late or "forgetting" the anniversary. Birthdays and Mother's Day weren't as bad, but I was late on a couple of those as well.

I was also guilty of reckless eyeballing. Many times, we would be out somewhere, and I would check out a chick or two. I thought it was something every man did, but I guess I was more disrespectful. I wouldn't just look, I would check out the whole package. After these things, and a few infidelities, my wife had had enough.

After a good night—I mean without any fighting or arguing— I went to work the next morning feeling good. We had been up and down a little, so it was good to feel like things were going in the right direction. I texted my wife from work like I always did. We exchanged texts, and something or the other was said. I can't recall what, but I got upset. To be honest, I probably overreacted. Nevertheless, I told her I was leaving work so we could talk. She refused, and told me stay at work. When I told her I would be home soon, she told me she wouldn't be there (it was a Saturday, so she wasn't at work, and I knew she would be there anyway). But that didn't go over too well with me. *How dare you tell me to stay at work? And you better be there when I get there.* Now, to be honest, I don't know if I said these things to her, but I know they were running through my head.

I told my supervisor I wasn't feeling well and I needed to go home. He allowed me to leave with no problem. I hopped in my Tahoe and took off toward my house. I just kept asking myself what she was thinking. *Why was she talking to me like that?* Well, it didn't matter because I was home and I would settle this. When I walked into the house yelling her name, I didn't get a response. I yelled again as I headed toward the bedroom. Aggressively pushing the door open, I discovered no one was home. Now I was really pissed off. *So you really did leave,* I thought. I hopped back in my truck and went to her parents' house, *where she better be,* I thought to myself. I called to let her know I was headed over there. She was hesitant at first, then agreed to turn a couple of corners with me so we could talk.

I pulled up about two minutes later, fuming! She got in and smiled, but I wasn't smiling. I was angry! I drove off and started talking very aggressively to her. I drove a couple of blocks, and she told me if I didn't calm down, she was getting out. I was tired of her telling me what she was or wasn't going to do. But to my surprise, she wasn't going to listen to me yell and be aggressive. She then told me to let her out of the car. I told her she wasn't going anywhere, so she opened the door. I grabbed her arm, telling her not to get out. As I rolled up to a stop sign, trying to decide if I should just run it so she couldn't get out or if I should stop, (well, I tried to just roll through the stop sign without stopping, so she couldn't get out with the car moving), I was wrong. She jumped out while the car was still moving. This was very out of character for her. Confused and angry, I headed home.

I tried to call a couple of times on my way, but she wasn't answering any of my calls. I left my house and went to my parents' house to talk to my father. Any time I had an issue, I would talk to him to get advice. My pops told me to give her time and space. I heard him, but space wasn't what I wanted, so I went home. I figured I'd call around seven or eight if she wasn't home by then. Eight o'clock came around and she wasn't home yet. I called to see when she was coming home, and she told me she came to get some clothes for her and the boys, and she was going to stay the night at her parents' house.

That night, I had some time to reflect on that day and the days leading up to it. I really didn't find fault in myself. I did not feel as though I did anything that bad. Yes, I lost my temper (I've done that in the past), but I didn't put my hands on her. Before this day, I had control. I controlled our home, and when we fought, I ended up controlling that as well. Or so I thought. I would find out in a later conversation that she was just tired of my shit. A person could only take so much. It wasn't until that conversation that I realized how much I neglected her and her needs.

I thought I had lost control, but I never really had it. I watched my father be a real husband to my mother for years. When I looked at myself and the type of husband I had been, I was disappointed in myself. Yet, I hadn't taken the time to look at myself.

The following day was more of the same. She decided I needed another day to cool off, which just made me angrier. We talked some on the phone; I was nice and didn't show the anger I was really feeling. I promised to control my anger, and she agreed to come back the next day. We had a good first couple of days, but things got bad quick. After her third day back, we got into a big fight. I was so frustrated by this point that I punched a hole in the door. Well, three holes to be exact. She said that this was the last straw, and she was going to stay with her parents. I asked how long, but she didn't know. She grabbed a couple of things on her way out the door. I followed behind. I remember thinking that I messed up this time, and it would be at least another two or three days before she would come back.

Those two or three days turned into two weeks. I was getting worse. I left the house even less and didn't want to talk, either. I would speak to my homie Marcus, a pastor friend of mine, and of course, Pops. But at this point, I wasn't feeling right. I'd never felt this way. EVER. I missed my family and didn't know if they would be coming back. I missed the boys playing nerf basketball until one of them ran the other into the wall, and I had to stop them. I missed them fighting. I missed EVERYTHING! I was alone without a partner. We had been through a lot together, but it looked like the end.

The house was so quiet now. All I could hear was myself think. That wasn't good. See, I hadn't figured out that I was the problem. So all this thinking just made me more upset. I reached an all-time low, however, I NEVER wanted to end my life. I was confused as to what my next move was a lot of the time, but I repeat, I never wanted to commit suicide.

My parents did what they could to help. They called every day and tried to get me to come over. Because of the relationship I had with my parents, it was easy for me to go to their house and discuss my problems with them. I did, on occasion. It helped. It helped me to just get out of the house. We would also talk about old times. My parents are good about being there whenever we need them. However, that joy was short-lived when I went back home to the darkness. To be honest, I didn't mind the darkness and alone time.

I believe a month had passed since we had been separated. I was doing nothing one afternoon when my wife called. I didn't hear a lot of excitement in her voice, but she didn't sound angry either. This had to be a good thing. She continued with some small talk, then asked if we could meet at my parents' house. It was odd, but I didn't ask why. I just agreed and headed that way. I called my dad and told him I was on the way over. I showed up after a shower and shave and told my parents how we were going to meet there and talk. My parents probably figured out what was going on, but I didn't. I was excited, thinking we were about to get back together, and she just wanted to lay down some ground rules. She told me she would be there after work, so I patiently awaited her arrival.

When she got there, I got a different vibe. She was different. She walked in with her parents, which also made me a little uncomfortable. She asked me to get my parents so we all could talk. I did, and we all sat down in the living room. She didn't waste any time talking. She started by saying how unhappy she was and had been for a long time. She brought up my temper. But to be honest, I don't remember much more after she asked for a divorce. I realize now this was why she wanted her parents and my parents there when she told me. My recent behavior must have made her think I would overreact. I think, more than that, her mind was made up and she wasn't going to give me a chance to change her mind.

After about half an hour of me asking why and if we could work it out, and her repeatedly telling me no and adding explanations as to why she wanted a divorce, I decided to get some air and went to the front porch, I must admit that I was lost and confused more than ever. It was tough living without my family, but I always thought we would get back together, and my family would come back home. Now it seemed like the end, and I really didn't know how to handle it. I stayed at my parents' house for a while that night, talking with my mom and dad, who seemed as surprised as I was. Then I went home to think and to be alone.

Chapter 23. Real Change?

My boys didn't want to stay with me. They wanted to be with their mothers. I was okay with that, or that's what I told them. I would pick them up from school or practice and take them to their mother's house. I have to be honest; it was killing me. They didn't want to be with me. I just didn't get it.

The house was almost empty. Well, my wife came and took most of her things and most of the boys' things to her mother's house. Anything she didn't want, she left at the house as storage. We spoke every day, but she was still firm with me. Not a lot of joking or playing around, straight to the point. I was cool with that because she could have just given me the cold shoulder and not talked to me at all.

She called one day and told me she still had a couple of things she needed to pick up from the house and that she would be by after work to pick the stuff up. I agreed, thinking I was going to get her to talk. In my mind, I still didn't know the "real" reason why she wanted a divorce. I couldn't help but think about what I was going to say. I knew I had to be gentle because she would shut down otherwise. So after running a hundred scenarios in my head, she called and said she was on her way over. I still didn't know how I was going to get her to open up and talk to me.

She showed up about five minutes later. I immediately greeted her with a big smile and a hug. She was accepting but not really enthused. She proceeded into the house to gather more of her and the kids' belongings. She stacked some totes and a couple of bags by the door. She made one more trip into the bedroom to get more clothes before she left. This was my opportunity to ask for a few minutes of her time. She didn't hesitate.

She walked toward the couch to sit down. I thought this would be good, even if I was a little confused. Why was she there to get more of her things if we were going to work it out? She never said that's what would happen, but that's what I thought.

We sat down right next to each other, and she immediately went in. She asked if I knew why she was divorcing me. I said because of my temper. She said no. I was confused, but I didn't have time to think. She continued by saying it was more than that. She asked if I remembered when her brother passed and if I remember where I was. I said yes, the funeral. She responded swiftly with a no. Her voice was now a little firmer.

"You went to the Derby. You went to the visitation, but you went to the Derby on the day of the funeral when I needed you the most."

It was an instant blow. I felt bad. But it had just begun. She didn't give me time to stop her flow of heartbreaking words. She asked me if I knew how many anniversaries, birthdays, Mother's Days, Valentine's Days I missed or was late for.

"Do you even know what day our anniversary is?" she said. She then asked if I knew how many times I missed holidays with her family. Or better yet, how many times did I show up for a holiday with her family? She talked about how much I "checked out" other women, and how embarrassing it was to have your man turn his head to check out women while he was with his wife. She ended with, "I was just waiting on you to cheat again, and I was going to leave you."

I didn't know what to say. When she finished talking, I felt about an inch tall. The room was quiet. I had to think of something, so I told her I would change, and she would see it. She said okay and got up off the couch to leave. I wanted to stop her, to tell her something, but I had no words. I told her goodbye and that I loved her. She said the same as she headed toward the door.

Once she left, I had time to let everything settle. I had to look at *me*. All the things she said about me were true. I loved my wife, but I didn't always show it. I thought I was a loving husband. I thought that because my wife didn't complain, everything was okay. The most important thing I learned from that conversation was that I needed real change. If I was ever going to get her back, I was going to have to change how I thought.

I started with where I went wrong. Being self-centered was the problem. I wasn't thinking about my wife; I was only thinking about myself. But why? I realized when I was in the streets, I had to protect *me*. I had homies who had been shot, robbed, carjacked, pistol-whipped, and even killed, being in the streets like I was. That made me put up a barrier that protected me from everyone else. I have to admit that with the success I had and the type of money that was coming in, I felt on top of the world, though. Don't get me wrong, there were guys getting more than me, but I bought what I wanted when I wanted. I went where I wanted when I wanted. I had more money and freedom than I could have ever imagined. I lived it up. But my guard was always up. I only trusted my team and a few associates. The streets made me a certain way, but *I* let it.

I've said before, I watched my father be a real husband to my mother for over thirty years. I was raised with morals and values. I let the streets change who I was. I became "B Money." I dove into the streets like I did basketball. I thought I was running a Fortune 500 weed company. But this guy, "B Money," couldn't be a loving husband. He didn't know how to put his wife's needs before his own. He didn't know how to do much more than provide and protect. I thought because I wasn't in the streets, I wasn't thinking the same way anymore. I was wrong.

I knew after this talk I was going to have to get it together. I had really messed things up. This wasn't going to be any easy fix, but I realized I was the problem, and I also realized how to fix it. I had to pay more attention to my wife's needs. I used to laugh when people would ask how she did it with a house full of boys. I never thought she was outnumbered, and maybe she needed some time away from the gym. Or maybe I should have just been more attentive. I guess you could say I had a moment of clarity. An epiphany.

Over the next couple of weeks, I started to pay attention to my wife. I was trying to be the husband I should have been the whole time we were married. I know it was only a couple of weeks, but my time alone was used to fix me. Once I realized why I became the way I did, I began to write. I was still depressed, and writing became a form of therapy for me.

My emotions were all over the place. I felt bad for the way I behaved in my relationship with my wife. At the same time, I realized why I was that way. I figured since I knew the problem, I could fix it and everything would go back to normal. It was working. Or so I thought. My wife seemed to be letting her guard down a little more around me. Between all my prayers, my actions, and my "therapy," I thought I was getting it together. And I was. However, I thought there was a quick fix to my problem. I'd done years of damage, and it couldn't be fixed in just a couple of weeks.

I decided to check my mail on a sunny Friday morning. I just made myself some bacon and eggs. Since I hadn't checked in a week, there was a lot of mail, but there were some bigger than normal envelopes. Of course, I went for those first. These letters came from a lawyer. A divorce lawyer. I looked closely at the name, and it looked familiar. I didn't know the attorney personally, but I'd heard nothing but good things about her. So, not only was I getting a divorce, but I was getting divorce papers from one of the best in the city. She wasn't playing either. She had my child support lined out, along with everything my wife wanted and what I could keep. After reading these papers, I felt defeated. I thought things were getting better. I thought I was showing how I could be a different person. It was too late.

I had to get an explanation. I called my wife and told her I received the papers. We both got quiet. I proceeded to ask why a lawyer and why her? She basically told me she was playing roulette and just picked one. She also said she got a lawyer because she thought it would be easier than dealing with me herself. I wouldn't say it out loud, but I agreed with her. Without arguing, I got off the phone and really started to do some thinking.

I didn't know now if I wanted to fight for my marriage. I wanted to throw in the towel. I don't believe in staying together for the kids. If it was not going to work, then we needed to move on. My boys were getting older, and I missed them more than anything. But I wanted to be happy, and I wanted my wife to be happy. And how could the kids be happy if we weren't happy? So, while still trying to be a better husband/father, I was more concerned with myself than anything now.

I learned a lot about myself. . I learned a lot about life. My time spent alone, while painful at first, was much needed. I needed to learn. Not just how to treat my wife, but about life. I don't know if I would have ever learned these things about myself that I never saw before if I didn't have this time to myself.

Chapter 24. Last Chapter

Before writing this book, I would have said that I've had it rough, just one bad break after another. In actuality, that's not true. I think back to basketball and the bad break I suffered on the court. Was it a bad break? Yes. I broke both bones in my arm, and even to this day, I can't open my hand all the way. But did I work as hard as I could to come back and play? No, I didn't.

My time on the streets was very profitable, but when I decided to leave the streets alone, I used to think about the losses I took, especially the last one. I couldn't figure out how I had all this money and a few months later, I had to get a job. Probably because I thought I could live the same life I was living when I was hustling. Then I got some property. The man I bought the property from told me how to get the house paid off sooner. He sat me down and gave me a blueprint. I refused to pay attention to it.

Ever since I broke my arm, I thought my life was one bad break after another. But in reality, I didn't look at myself. All I can remember is not giving a f*ck about anything after I broke my arm. I inserted myself into the streets. I don't know what it was about the streets, but from the early ages of chilling on Liberty with my uncle to my own time as a real player on the streets, I LOVED IT. I know now that this is why I became the person I became. Although I knew better, I wanted to be on the streets. I wanted to hustle like some of the OG's I'd seen. I jumped into a game I didn't know anything about. I learned the game from the OG's and just being on the streets. But when you move up the food chain, things change. When I was buying cocaine, I bought it from a homeboy of mine. But when I started moving twenty-five to fifty pounds, I was going with the connect to pick up fifty to two hundred. We were riding with over fifty thousand dollars at the very least. (And that's the trip down. On the way back, we were riding with fifty to two hundred pounds of weed. I wasn't dealing with a homeboy anymore. I was dealing with someone I didn't even know. I made the trip by myself during a couple of droughts. However, at this point, I had to really protect myself. And I did. This was where I built my wall and became emotionless for a long time.

And although I wasn't in the streets, I never changed my mentality. I thought about *me* and protecting *me*. I never gave up wanting to live that life, either.

I threw a comedy show. It was a great show. All I had to do was stick to it. Put on another show and do some things different from the last one. I didn't do that either.

What about my personal life? I lost my wife and kids. The loss of my family changed me forever. It caused me to suffer from depression and anxiety. But it also caused me to take a long look at myself.

My time spent alone is what helped me understand why I was the way I was. I had time to really look at myself. I mean *really* look at myself and be honest about my life. I had to give myself the brutal truth. That was hard. But once I changed my mentality, I was able to change.

I allowed things to consume me. I didn't have any balance. I threw myself into the streets after I broke my arm. I then threw myself into coaching and my boys. I made a lot of mistakes, and some I wish I could take back. However, if asked if I would do it all again to receive the same results, I'd say, "Yes." If going through what I went through ensured that my oldest two sons got to college and my third son had the opportunity to go to college, without them selling drugs, then yes! I would do it all over.